A Found Joy

Crawdad Beach Series (Book 11)

Lisa Buffaloe

A Found Joy

Visit the author's website at https://lisabuffaloe.com.

Cover Design: JoAnn Durgin

A Found Joy

Laughter and love filled Hannah Joy's childhood. However, on her twenty-first birthday, her life takes a dramatic turn when she discovers family secrets that put her at risk. Seeking safety, Hannah flees to the anonymity of Crawdad Beach, where she hopes and prays to find the truth surrounding her past.

Cameron Doss enjoyed success, friendships, family, and a bright future until a devious relationship shattered his world. When his aunt offers him a job in Crawdad Beach, Cameron jumps at the opportunity to escape the lies and deceit that wrecked his life.

Hannah and Cameron must confront their past, but will they find healing and their faith strengthened, or will their discoveries destroy their future?

Book 11 of the Crawdad Beach Series

Readers may enjoy each book in the series as a standalone novel.

"Although my father and my mother have abandoned me, yet the Lord will take me up and adopt me as His child." For "God is a father of the fatherless" (Psalm 27:10, AMP, Psalm 68:5).

Therefore, "Do not call to mind the former things, or consider things of the past. Behold, I am going to do something new, now it will spring up; will you not be aware of it? I will even make a roadway in the wilderness, rivers in the desert."
(Isaiah 43:18-19, NASB)

Table of Contents

Chapter 1

The insistent buzzing of Hannah Joy's alarm vibrated on top of her nightstand. She rolled over and slapped her phone app to silence the irritating noise.

With a groan, she threw the covers over her head. Why wasn't it the weekend so she could sleep in today? Why did she have to go to work?

"Happy twenty-first birthday," she mumbled to the empty room.

Hannah sat on the edge of her bed. Pale, early morning light filtered through the slats of her window blinds, making a striped pattern on the old, worn carpeting.

Mama D would tell her to count her blessings. Hannah stood and stretched her back. She was blessed with a job and a place to live, but there were many things she wished were different, so many aspects of her life felt incomplete.

The unopened cards sitting on Hannah's nightstand drew her attention. At least there was something to open on her birthday. She took the cards with her as she shuffled to the kitchen and started her coffee pot.

Comforted by the aroma of brewing coffee, Hannah

sat in the worn plastic chair beside the rickety card table that served as her dining area.

She smiled as she opened the first card from Dorthea Samson, who everyone called Mama D. The sweet woman, now older and more frail, had moved six months ago to live with her son in South Carolina. The faint scent of her perfume still clung to the paper, a comforting reminder of the woman Hannah considered her true mother.

Mama D's skin tone reminded Hannah of honey and chocolate—sweet, refreshing, and soothing. The precious woman had given her a loving home, treated her like family, taught her about Jesus, homeschooled her, and helped her get a cosmetologist's license.

Hannah didn't even know she was a white girl until she was five, when a neighbor told her the truth. Hannah had thought God hadn't put enough skin paint on her, and she'd grow into a deeper color.

Teary-eyed at the sweet words in Mama D's card, Hannah set it aside and picked up the one she was most curious about. Francesca Joy had sent Hannah a birthday card. She knew she should be grateful, but she barely knew the woman.

Maybe Hannah should have gone with Mama D when she moved to the south. She'd begged Hannah to join them. But she wanted to prove she could make it on her own, plus Francesca was in Pittsburgh some of the time.

Francesca had claimed to be Hannah's aunt, that her parents had died in a car wreck. Hannah believed her until her tenth birthday, when she overheard a conversation.

Mama D had told Francesca she would never lie to Hannah, and that Francesca needed to tell Hannah who she really was.

"You don't understand." Francesca's voice had quivered. "It's not up to me. I can't!" She stormed away and slammed the door behind her.

Later, when Hannah asked Mama D, she discovered the truth. Francesca was her mother.

But everyone pretended not to know.

Three months ago, Francesca invited Hannah to her townhouse. It was the first time she'd seen where her mother lived. The place looked like a showroom, nicely decorated but lacking any personal touches. No photos at all.

Even their conversation had been strange. Francesca had told Hannah to be careful and then asked if she needed anything, which was even more odd, since Francesca never seemed to care that much.

Shaking off her thoughts, Hannah opened the large decorative birthday card and read the nice sentiment about happy birthday wishes that could have come from anyone.

Nestled within the larger envelope was a smaller one containing a key, bank account number, and a handwritten note.

Hannah, go <u>today</u> to the bank that I took you to on your sixteenth birthday; the one downtown with the towering columns and marble floor. The documents you signed that day weren't only for your savings account, but also to give you access to my safe deposit box.
Be careful.

Chapter 2

Why did Francesca want her to be careful?

Clutching the straps of her backpack, Hannah stood in the bank vault, the silence broken only by the teller's rattling keys as she worked to open the safe deposit box.

The teller handed Hannah the big, long, rectangular metal container that belonged to Francesca. Hannah followed the lady to a small private room and waited until the door was closed.

Hannah needed to hurry. Her beauty shop boss was not happy about her calling in and saying she would be late. She didn't have a client scheduled for another hour, but that didn't matter to her boss. Although employee pay was commission-based, a full day's work was expected of everyone.

Opening the safe deposit box, Hannah removed a legal-sized white envelope bearing the name of a law office. Francesca's will was inside. The will, written only three months ago, left everything to Hannah and named her as the executor.

Hannah stared at the legal document. What did that mean? Francesca was only forty-two. Why did she have a will? Did she find out she had cancer, some terrible illness, or have a premonition that something bad would happen? Is that why she told Hannah to be careful?

A prickling sensation on the back of her neck made her look over her shoulder at the closed door. Mama D would tell her to remember Bible verses about God not giving us the spirit of fear, and the other one about God never leaving or forsaking us.

The verses running through Hannah's mind steadied her breathing. Another envelope contained a printout of bank statements that showed the activity on Francesca's account for the last six months.

There were no checks listed, no credit card payments, and nothing that showed a mortgage was being paid. The only activity was a monthly amount deposited from the company where Francesca worked, along with a series of withdrawals.

Three months ago, $157,000 had been in the account. Now there was only $243.07. What did Francesca do with all that money?

Reaching inside the box again, Hannah pulled out a packet of photos. As far as she knew, Francesca didn't keep pictures of herself, Hannah, or anyone else in her townhouse. Is this where Francesca hid them?

The first group of pictures featured Francesca— young, smiling, standing next to a man and a woman in a sunny, tropical locale with an ocean backdrop.

Francesca's various ages in the photographs from childhood revealed that they spanned many years. Were these photos taken in France, where Francesca said she grew up?

Hannah leaned closer, her eyes scanning the details. There were similarities between the couple and Francesca. Perhaps they were relatives or Hannah's maternal grandparents. But that didn't make sense since Francesca said they died when Francesca was a little girl.

Laying the photos aside, Hannah opened a sealed, plain envelope. A paper with a copy of Hannah's baby picture had the words in Francesca's elegant handwriting.

This is your daughter, Mon amour.

Hannah gulped, her throat dry and tight. Francesca said that Hannah's father had died before her birth. Had that been a lie?

The next pack of photos was of Hannah as a little girl, spanning from about six months old to the present. Had Mama D been giving them to Francesca? Why were they kept hidden?

Next were newspaper clippings showing a man and Francesca at charity functions around the world. Based on the articles, Francesca was the personal assistant to Johan Rauchmann, the owner of Rauchmann Industries. The company had offices worldwide, including its U.S.

headquarters in Pittsburgh. Hannah knew Francesca worked at that company, but she'd never seen a photo of Johan.

Another photo showed Francesca wearing an elegant evening dress, her light brown hair pulled up in a stylish bun. She stood next to Johan. The handsome older man wore a tuxedo. Streaks of gray highlighted the dark hair at his temples; his intense green eyes held a captivating, yet unnerving, gaze.

The man's dark hair and green eyes were just like Hannah's.

Icy fingers slithered up her spine.

Was that her father?

With trembling hands, Hannah opened another envelope to find birth certificates—one hers, the other Francesca's — showing they were born in the same town in South Carolina. No, that couldn't be right. Francesca spoke French and said she'd grown up in Paris. Hannah grew up in the Pittsburgh area. She never thought she'd been born anywhere other than Pennsylvania.

How could she not have known? Then again, she'd never asked.

Hannah's father was listed as unknown. Feeling a headache start behind her eyes, she rubbed her forehead. Why hadn't she seen her birth certificate before? Her homeschooling meant she didn't need one. The only time she remembered the document being used was when

Francesca took her to get her driver's license and handed it to the lady at the DMV.

Did Francesca have Hannah's birth certificate when she opened the savings account? She couldn't remember. Were all the things she thought she knew about herself and Francesca nothing but carefully constructed lies?

Another manila envelope was next. Hannah pulled out statements for a savings account in her name. It now contained $185,845.12.

What?

How could that be possible?

Had Francesca transferred money into Hannah's account? Why would she do that?

One small piece of paper remained at the bottom of the safe deposit box.

Hannah's vision blurred, the elegant loops of her mother's handwriting swimming before her eyes.

I'm so sorry, Hannah. So very sorry. Please forgive me. This was not the life I wanted for either of us.

I love you. I always have, and I always will. I love you forever.

Your loving mother, Francesca

Chapter 3

Her mother loved her? Why didn't Francesca ever admit that fact to Hannah and tell her sooner?

Gripping the steering wheel, Hannah drove back to her apartment to store the documents. She couldn't take them to work with her. Not with all the nosy beauticians who worked there.

Sadness and anger warred within as she processed what she'd found. Regardless of the discoveries, the fact remained that she had a great childhood filled with love and laughter. Mama D and her family embraced Hannah as one of their own.

When she first discovered that Francesca was her mother, Hannah sobbed uncontrollably for days. Not because of the things she'd missed or that Francesca never claimed Hannah as her own, but the horrifying thought of having to leave Mama D's loving home.

Focusing on the road ahead, questions swirled in Hannah's mind. How many lies had Francesca told? Who were the people in the photos? Could the couple in the pictures with Francesca be Hannah's grandparents? Were they still alive?

What was she supposed to do with the money that was now in her account?

What if the green-eyed man was her father, Johan Rauchmann, the steel tycoon? Was Hannah Johan's love child with Francesca? Hannah cringed at the thought, but she knew some things about her mother.

Other teenagers got in trouble for taking drugs, doing something illegal, or immoral. Francesca hadn't approved of Hannah becoming a Christian, which was another thing that made little sense. Why had Francesca chosen the sweetest Christian woman ever to raise Hannah, if Francesca didn't want Christianity rubbing off on her daughter?

An interesting thought took root. Mama D often talked about the sovereignty of God, that as the heavens are higher than the earth, so are God's ways and thoughts higher than ours. Only God knows everything. What if God gifted Hannah with Mama D? Hannah's salvation aside, the woman was the best gift she'd ever received.

Hannah parked her car and leaned over the steering wheel, checking to ensure no one was loitering in the parking lot. Mama D had disapproved of Hannah's choice of apartments. It wasn't her brightest idea, but it had been available when she needed it, and kept her praying.

The wind sent an empty beer can skittering across the cracked pavement. With the coast clear, Hannah grabbed her backpack. She locked her car behind her, ran up the stairs to her apartment, unlocked the door, hurried inside, relocked it, and slid the chain into place.

Safely inside, Hannah put her backpack on the card table and slumped onto the plastic chair. She glanced around her sparsely furnished apartment.

Why was she coming back here? Francesca might be at her townhouse. Hannah grabbed her backpack and locked her apartment behind her. She needed answers.

Arriving at Francesca's townhouse, Hannah parked in the driveway. The sports car wasn't there, which wasn't surprising. It might be in the garage, but Francesca was probably already at work. Still, it was worth a try to see if she was home.

Hannah made her way up the sidewalk. When she visited a few months ago, Francesca gave Hannah a key to the townhouse and the security code. Could that visit, plus all the information in the safe deposit box, be laying the groundwork for a true mother-daughter relationship? And if so, why now?

Curious about the thought, Hannah found the note where she'd written the security information. She punched in the code on the keypad next to the door.

A shrill beep announced that her entry was incorrect. Maybe she didn't put it in the right way.

She tried again. It still didn't work.

Did Francesca change the code since Hannah visited?

With deliberate movements, she slowly and carefully

typed it in again.

A shrill, insistent beep ripped through the silence, announcing the alarm's displeasure.

Hannah inserted the key into the lock. It wouldn't turn.

She double-checked to make sure she was holding the key correctly and tried again.

No luck.

Hannah walked to the front window and peeked through the blinds.

Shock jolted her as she stared at the empty room.

Everything was gone.

Someone had neatly vacuumed the carpeted floor, as though no one lived there.

Hannah ran to the garage and jumped up so she could see through the top windows. The car was also gone.

Who would have taken everything? Or did Francesca leave without even saying goodbye?

A sick feeling washed over Hannah. Was that why Francesca sent the birthday card and told Hannah to go to the bank?

What if something terrible had happened? Gasping for air, Hannah doubled over, her hands on her knees, chest heaving.

She had to think. Maybe someone at Francesca's work would know where she went. Then again, was it even possible to gain access to the company?

Francesca never took Hannah to her workplace. Not even once.

No one probably knew Hannah even existed.

Chapter 4

Where had Francesca gone?

The whine of hair dryers and the smell of hairspray filled the air as Hannah tried to concentrate on cutting her client's hair.

Her boss was furious that Hannah had missed her first appointment. It wasn't as if she could explain her morning or why she was two hours late.

She'd tucked the documents away in her apartment closet, but felt like they were a lightning rod for something bad to happen.

Her mother's townhouse had been cleaned out, her car was gone, and she was missing. Did Francesca fly off with her lover or run away from Hannah? Or was something more disturbing going on?

Hannah grimaced. Should she have called the police and reported a robbery at the townhouse? No, she couldn't do that because she didn't know what really had happened.

In her call to Mama D, she had pleaded with Hannah to leave her job and move to South Carolina, suggesting that she either live with her, settle nearby, or move to

Crawdad Beach, where Mama D's cousin lived.

Hannah wasn't ready to leave and go anywhere. Not now. Not until she figured out where Francesca had gone.

"Excuse me."

Pausing her scissors, Hannah focused on the brown-haired woman sitting in the beautician's chair. "Yes?"

"Could you stop cutting? I'd like to have a little hair left."

Heat rocketed to Hannah's face. "I'm so sorry." She set down her scissors and dried her client's hair. Hopefully, she'd be able to tease and poof her hair to give it some volume.

By the time she finished, the lady was happy and even left her a big tip.

For the rest of the day, Hannah stayed busy and tried not to think about anything but giving her clients the care they needed.

By three o'clock, Hannah had finished for the day. She cleaned up her station, then went to the dingy back room to rest her feet. The smell of stale coffee, cigarette smoke, and old pizza hung in the air.

Maybe her boss would let her go home.

"Hey, Hannah banana," the gravelly-voiced beautician walked into the room and poured a cup of coffee. "What kept you this morning?"

Hannah shrugged. "I had to take care of a couple of things." There was no way she would give details, since gossip spread like gangrene in the place.

Reeking of cigarette smoke, the woman sat at the table across from her. "I saw something in the online news this morning and wondered if you knew the person." She clicked open her cellphone and scrolled through before turning the screen toward Hannah. "Did you know her?"

Hannah leaned in to get a closer look.

A fatality occurred Thursday night when a vehicle veered off the Parkway East outbound close to the Squirrel Hill Tunnel. Law enforcement, emergency services, and the Allegheny County Medical Examiner's Office responded to the incident.

The driver, Francesca Joy of Pittsburgh, was pronounced dead on the scene. The absence of skid marks led police to conclude that Ms. Joy had fallen asleep while driving.

Hannah's vision blurred as the room swam.
Her mother was dead.

Chapter 5

Francesca was dead.

Hot tears streamed down Hannah's face, her shoulders shaking with grief for all that she didn't have in a relationship with her mother and the questions Hannah would never get answered.

Aware of the muted and whispered conversations behind her, Hannah vaulted out of her chair, grabbed her coat, and ran to her car.

For twenty-one years, Francesca never admitted she was Hannah's mother. Why did Francesca leave her in the care of Mama D? Who does that kind of thing? And why?

Why had Francesca waited to admit she was Hannah's mother through papers in a safe deposit box?

Hannah drove onto the freeway and turned toward her apartment. What was she going to do now?

Francesca was gone, and Mama D moved.

Hannah didn't have anyone.

Her cell phone rang. She didn't want to talk. Not now. It was probably the beauty shop wondering where she had gone.

The thought of going back to that place made her

crazy. The job paid her bills, but the other stylists were catty and mean.

If Francesca died last night, who had already moved her belongings from the townhouse? Had Francesca taken everything because she was leaving? Or had it been someone else?

Hannah exited the freeway and turned her car toward Francesca's townhouse. She needed to find out the truth. Maybe a neighbor knew what happened.

Forty-five minutes later, Hannah sat in her apartment as Francesca's neighbor's words echoed in Hannah's mind.

I thought it was strange Francesca wasn't there when the movers were working. So I went over and asked them. They said Francesca's house, car, and belongings were all leased, and the company was reclaiming its property.

A shiver ran down Hannah's spine as the hair on the back of her neck stood on end. The company took her mom's things? Was that even legal? What if something bad was going on?

Hannah called Mama D to share the unsettling news.

"Baby, you have *got* to get out of there," Mama D's voice urged. "I have a bad feeling about this. I spent most of the night praying for your protection. Come to South Carolina."

Hannah rubbed her hand through her hair. "But what

about Francesca? Don't I need to go to a funeral home and take care of...things?"

A long, heavy silence hung on the call. "I don't know, baby. I guess you could call the police and find out where they took your mother."

Hannah shuddered. Why did she have to do that by herself?

Mama D kept reassuring her that God would be with her.

But why wasn't God there with skin on, holding her hand?

An hour later, Hannah took a deep breath, opened the funeral home door, and stepped into a brightly lit foyer.

A middle-aged woman sat behind a polished wood receptionist's desk, looked up, and smiled. "May I help you?"

Hannah gripped her backpack strap. "Yes. I, uh, need to talk to someone about my mother, who died, Francesca Joy."

"I'm very sorry for your loss." The woman pointed to the seating area. "One of our staff will be right out." Picking up the landline phone receiver, the woman whispered something into the receiver.

Feeling like she was trapped inside a bad dream, Hannah perched on the edge of the chair and rubbed her forehead.

A young woman with auburn hair, her face flushed, hurried toward her. "You're here about Francesca Joy?"

"Yes, I need to make the arrangements."

A strange, almost imperceptible flicker of uncertainty crossed her face before a slow nod. "I'm Sandy Goodson. And you are?"

"Hannah Joy. Her daughter."

"I see." Sandy's gaze flickered toward the receptionist; a silent, knowing glance passed between them. "Follow me."

Hannah trailed behind the woman as they walked down a corridor. To the left, rows of identical offices with their doors closed; to the right, the area was open to a glassed-in outdoor atrium.

Sandy motioned to the chairs facing her desk and waited until Hannah took a seat. "Ms. Joy, the arrangements for Francesca have already been taken care of. There's nothing you need to worry about."

"I don't understand. How can that be? I'm her only daughter."

For a split second, shock registered on Sandy's face before she regained a placid expression. She opened a folder filled with documents. "Per Francesca's wishes, she was cremated and her ashes transported overseas."

The lady at the funeral home tried to make it sound like it was a good thing that Francesca's arrangements had already been made. But who had done that? Who sent her mother's ashes overseas, and why?

No matter what questions Hannah asked, nothing made sense.

The shocking numbness lingered as she drove back to her place. Hannah hit the steering wheel. Why couldn't she wake up from this nightmare?

Wait a minute. She now had money in the bank, cash in her purse, and had transferred a substantial amount into a checking account. She could start a new life in South Carolina.

There wasn't anything left for her here.

Not now.

Francesca was gone, not just absent, but as if someone deliberately erased her from existence.

A creepy feeling crawled up Hannah's spine as she pulled into her apartment parking lot.

What if her mother's death wasn't an accident? What if they took her things to erase the evidence?

Hannah's skin prickled. What if they came after her?

She checked to make sure the coast was clear, ran to her apartment, locked the door, and rushed to get her laptop. She had to get away.

Where was that place Mama D told her about? Crawdad something? Crawdad Beach. That was it. Hannah searched the internet.

Photos of a cute little town filled her screen. There was even a beauty shop. Yes. Maybe they would hire her.

Hannah checked the cosmetology licensing requirements by state. She should be fine going to South Carolina. What else would she need?

First, quit her job here. She dreaded the prospect of going in person. Perhaps since her mother passed away, her boss would be understanding.

Hannah placed the call. After it was over, she went to the bathroom to take antacid tablets. The conversation with her boss went far worse than she'd expected. All the lady did was curse Hannah out for leaving without giving notice.

She slumped in her chair. What else could she do? Maybe she could get letters of recommendation from some of her clients to send to her email account. Hannah called her two closest female clients.

Thankfully, those conversations went well, and they agreed to email recommendation letters to her inbox.

While she waited for their replies, Hannah searched the internet to find information about Johan Rauchmann. It didn't take long to discover that the man had one son and had been married to the same woman for forty-three years.

Hannah scrolled through the photos of Johan and his family. His wife was a beautiful, dignified blonde with striking blue eyes that seemed to stare right at her.

Why would Johan be married to such a beautiful woman and still want a mistress? Maybe that's why all traces of Francesca's belongings were removed from the townhouse. Hannah swallowed hard as goosebumps rose on her arms.

Whoever took Francesca's things, whether it was Johan or someone else, probably would want to erase an illegitimate offspring.

Hannah crossed to the window and peered out through the slats of her blinds. She recognized the beat-up Honda Civic, the dented pickup truck, the black sedan, and the minivan that usually parked near her building. She hadn't seen the dark gray car with tinted windows before. Was someone sitting inside?

She backed away and ran to her bedroom. Her one suitcase would not be enough. She threw all her clothes and shoes onto her bed and wrapped them in her sheets and bedspread.

Hurrying to the kitchen, she grabbed plastic grocery bags to use for anything else she wanted to take. It wasn't worth taking her furniture.

But what about her rent? She'd already paid this month, but she needed to get to the office to pay the cleaning fee and termination money. Whatever they wanted, it wouldn't matter.

She had to get away.

Chapter 6

With a cautious breath, Hannah peered out her window blinds. The unfamiliar car was still there. The dark-tinted windows kept her from seeing whether anyone was inside.

If someone were watching, how could she get all her belongings out of the apartment? Hannah paced back and forth. It would take her several trips to stuff all her belongings into her vehicle.

She needed to get out of here. She didn't want to wait until it was night, but how could she do that without being seen?

A memory of a prayer Mama D had prayed years ago came to mind. They had accidentally driven into a bad part of town and stopped at a streetlight. While waiting for the light to turn green, a group of men walked toward them, staring in a way that made them feel very uneasy.

Mama D had prayed out loud that just as Jesus healed a man born blind, He would make the men blind to their presence. After Mama D prayed, the men turned and walked away.

Some would dismiss it as a coincidence. Hannah

knew better. God had protected them.

Hoping God was listening, Hannah looked up at the ceiling. "God, I really need your help. If there are people out there watching me, would you please put blinders on their eyes so they can't see me?"

It took her only twenty minutes to load her belongings into her car. Hannah slammed her foot on the gas. The overloaded vehicle lurched forward and died.

"Okay, Nellie, we've got a long way to go." She patted the dashboard. "You can do it. We've got to get out of here. Only 600 miles, and we'll be in Crawdad Beach."

She'd made the trip to South Carolina one other time when she carried Mama D to live with her son. Sending up another prayer for help, Hannah tried starting the car again. The engine sputtered and coughed before finally settling into a somewhat rhythmic pattern.

Hannah checked her GPS, its screen displaying a detailed map, and switched it on to guide her. For the long journey ahead, her phone's music app included a variety of genres, including soft rock, praise and worship, gospel songs, old Motown hits, movie orchestra soundtracks, and audiobooks.

She cranked up the music on her playlist, accelerated onto Interstate 79 South, and merged into traffic.

A monstrous wave of sound and wind buffeted her car as an eighteen-wheeler roared past.

Hannah changed lanes and matched the speed of the

white minivan in front of her. Stickers lined their back windshield, signifying the vehicle held a dad, mom, three kids, and a dog and cat.

An ache welled in Hannah's chest. She'd prayed for years for Francesca, but her mother said she found no need for a belief in God or Jesus. As far as Francesca was concerned, her life didn't require a higher power. She saw religion as a crutch for those who were weaker. And she despised weakness.

Knowing now what Hannah knew, Francesca probably hadn't wanted anything that might make her feel guilty about the life she led. So, why did she have a godly woman like Mama D raise Hannah? Mama D would say it was a God thing. Maybe it was.

A bright red Corvette Stingray zoomed past, followed by a sleek black Porsche 911. Hannah gripped the steering wheel. Everything Francesca owned was gone, including her fancy sports car.

Inhaling deeply, Hannah expelled the depressing thoughts. She could still hear Mama D's comforting voice. "Baby, grieve what you've lost. Let the tears fall, but remember not to get stuck in grief. Each day brings new chances and blessings from above with God-given possibilities."

Hannah nodded. She needed to remember that God was with her. He would see her through.

At least she hoped so.

If only her faith were as strong as Mama D's.

With the past in her rearview mirror, Hannah focused on the open road stretching before her.

The old was gone, and oh, how she hoped that new God-given possibilities were coming.

The rapid fire of nail guns, drone of generators, and a steady beat of hammers filled the air as Cameron Doss took a moment to calculate what he needed for a twelve-foot-long wall, ten feet high, with twelve-inch on-center stud spacing.

He double-checked his figures with the blueprint and gave himself a mental pat on the back. His friends used to complain during geometry, algebra, and calculus, but Cameron always enjoyed math and working with his hands.

His friends joked that his math skills were because of Cameron's partial Asian heritage. He didn't think it was heritage as much as the fact that his dad was a math teacher.

His aunt Katherine walked toward him and handed him a water bottle. "How's it going?" Katherine's long, dark hair was pulled back into a ponytail. Of all his aunts, Katherine, although taller and slimmer, bore the most resemblance to Cameron's late Asian grandmother.

"Thanks. It's going well." He took a swig of water. In the last four months, he'd learned more from his builder aunt than from any of his other jobs.

"I'm grateful you moved here to help." Katherine's smile was gentle.

Cameron glanced at the work crew around him. He knew the truth. He wasn't really needed. She'd given him an opportunity for a fresh start, a lifeline to escape the crushing weight of his problems.

Katherine surveyed the blueprints before returning her gaze to Cameron. "The spec homes are a nice change from my usual renovations."

"I think these houses will be a perfect size for new buyers or for people looking for something easier to maintain." If things had turned out differently, he would have been among the first to buy one.

"Now that you're here," Katherine grinned, "maybe I can finally convince that baby brother of mine to bring the rest of his family to South Carolina."

"I don't think that's going to happen. Dad's not moving anywhere if he can't get Texas barbecue and a good Mexican restaurant."

"You're probably right," his aunt chuckled, "but you never know what God might do next in Crawdad Beach."

Cameron gave her a nod, but inside, he wondered if even God could fix the mess he'd gotten into back in Texas.

Chapter 7

The bright optimism Hannah felt about leaving the past behind vanished far too quickly.

Between crying, screaming, ranting, and raving about the situation she was in, and the endless questions about Francesca, and what happened to her mother, Hannah had numerous conversations with God.

Well, actually, she did most of the talking.

Once Hannah calmed down and was quiet, Bible verses came to mind, soothing her like warm, comforting hugs. She remembered the Bible said God is a Father to the fatherless, and even if your father and mother abandon you, the Lord will adopt you as His child.

Mama D often reminded Hannah that who could have a better Father than a perfect, loving God? Hannah gave a quick, grateful glance heavenward before focusing again on the freeway.

She wasn't alone. God was her Father. He had adopted her. Plus, the sweetest woman on earth had raised her.

At Hannah's first stop, she gassed up her car, grabbed a bite to eat, and emailed her resume and letters of recommendation to Curl and Dye Beauty Shop in Crawdad Beach.

By the time she stopped again, the owner, Wanda King, had already sent Hannah her phone number with a request for an online interview, explaining that one of their beauticians had retired and they needed a quick replacement.

Shocked at the fast reply, Hannah placed the call. While she sat in her car, Wanda did the interview and hired Hannah on the spot, even sending her a link to a furnished duplex apartment available at a low rate.

After that surprise, Hannah's next phone call to Mama D was filled with happy squeals, culminating in a praise party since the quick hiring had to be a God thing. Because how would something like that happen otherwise?

Cameron parked his pickup in front of Doohickeys Hardware. Katherine sent him to retrieve the shipment of framing nails for their nail guns. He enjoyed being part of a ground-up project, starting a new subdivision. Plus, it gave him the opportunity to focus on something other than what had happened in Texas.

"Cameron," Sammie Banks, standing behind the counter, motioned with his chin. "I have Katherine's shipment in the back storage room."

"Thanks. I also wanted to buy a pair of work gloves. My other one had an unfortunate incident." Cameron avoided mentioning his unpleasant experience in the porta-potty. Putting his gloves in his back pocket before he took care of business had not been his brightest idea.

Sammie led him to the appropriate aisle. "How are things going on the job site?"

"Great. Katherine's floor plans are fantastic."

"It's funny. Growing up here, we didn't have many people leaving or moving into the area. Seems like in the last few years, people from all over are showing up in our little town, ready for a new start."

Cameron tried on a pair of gloves. "From what you told me about your wife, that turned out very well for you."

Sammie grinned as he twisted the wedding band on his finger. "River, showing up here was the best thing that ever happened to me. Besides Jesus. Maybe someone will show up that you find interesting."

"I'm not looking for a woman," Cameron growled as he removed the gloves. "No way. They'll rip your heart out, stomp on it, spit on it, run it through a meat grinder, and then smash it some more, then lie that you were the one to blame."

Sammie's eyebrows rose to his hairline. "Okay. Well, I'll be at the counter if you need me." He backed away and hurried down the aisle.

Cameron smacked the gloves against his jeans. He had to get a handle on his anger. He used to be an easygoing guy, but not anymore, not after what Ivy did to him.

At first, he loved the attention his gorgeous Texas girlfriend gave him. They met at work. She was in a different department. One day, he walked by her cubicle and noticed she'd dropped an apple. He gallantly scooped up the fruit, and the rest was history.

Ivy had posted photos of their time together online, bragging about her wonderful boyfriend. Within a few weeks of dating, she wanted to be with him only, spending as much time as possible together.

His parents voiced concern over Ivy's behavior, but Cameron loved his girlfriend's attention. That was until she became obsessive, controlling, and manipulative, putting a distance between him, his friends, and family.

When Cameron broke off their relationship, Ivy went nuts, hitting his chest and his face, and when she tried to knee him, he restrained her by holding her arms against her side.

He'd never forget the look she gave him. Her normally beautiful, big blue eyes turned to icy slits.

"You'll regret this," Ivy hissed, her voice a low, venomous whisper that sent a chill down his spine.

Within an hour, she had posted photos of herself on social media with her hair messed up and a big, vibrant bruise on her cheek, claiming he'd attacked her.

He *never* hit her and would never hit a woman. Yet, her scathing online posts and whispered accusations around the company poisoned his reputation and left him with no way to prove his innocence.

She then demanded payment for her "pain and suffering."

Instead, he hired a lawyer.

A week later, Cameron's truck was keyed, and his tires slashed.

The misery continued at work with whispered conversations behind his back, looks of disgust from the other women, and glares from some of the guys.

When his aunt offered Cameron a job and a place to live in one of her downtown loft apartments, he jumped at the opportunity.

He didn't need to have anything to do with women. Not now and not ever.

Chapter 8

Hannah grinned and shouted, Hallelujah! She'd made it to Crawdad Beach.

She let up on the gas, exhaled slowly, and relaxed her shoulders. All that worry was for nothing. God kept her safe, and now she was ready to see what He had in store for her.

A sign with a cute crawfish welcomed people to town. While she stopped at a blinking red light, she noted a gas station, a volunteer fire department, and a large white-steepled church. Hannah pulled into the empty parking lot to text Mama D that she'd arrived safely.

Back in Pennsylvania at Mama D's church, elderly saints filled the pews; their faces etched with years of faith and quiet dignity. Hannah loved the uplifting old hymns, powerful sermons, and the abundant kindness shown by the people who embraced her as one of their own.

She'd promised Mama D she'd find a church home when she arrived. For Mama D, Hannah would do anything.

She pulled back onto the road. With a groan of protesting metal, her overloaded car bumped across a rusty railroad track. An old train depot now housed a public library. Painted on the side was a cartoon crawdad reading a book while relaxing on the beach.

Maybe she could do that, too. Sit under a beach umbrella, the smell of salt and sunscreen in the air, and lose herself in a happy-ever-after book where moms and dads love and don't abandon their kids.

Hannah eased up her speed as she drove onto the brick pavement of Main Street. A cheerful pink and white awning sheltered the door of the Curl and Dye Beauty Shop.

Even though it was past business hours, the lights were still on. Parking in front, Hannah pushed open her car door. Thankfully, the temperature was much warmer than the chilly one she left behind in Pennsylvania.

She stretched her back until she felt a satisfying pop. Below the big windows of the beauty shop sat a vibrant collection of glazed ceramic pots, each brimming with flowers and greenery. Bright flowers adorned the second-floor balcony.

Hannah peeked inside the building. On the back wall was a drawing of a cute cartoon crawdad with curlers on its head, holding a hair dryer in one claw. Bright floral wallpaper graced the side walls of the salon. Gold-rimmed mirrors reflected a row of gleaming styling chairs.

Hopefully, in a few days, when she started at Curl and Dye, the other beauticians would be friendly, decent people.

Hannah loved meeting her clients and enjoyed creatively cutting and styling their hair. However, the last place she worked had way too much drama with the other stylists.

Besides that, the raunchy conversations the other beauticians discussed just about melted Hannah's ears off. They thought it was hilarious when she blushed. It wasn't just that her cheeks would heat; she felt like her brain was begging for a mind wash by the time she got off work.

Hannah returned to her car and continued checking out the area. The road curved around a community park with brightly colored playground equipment and a trail following a meandering, shallow river. The bright green leaves on the trees and blooming flowers showed that spring arrived much sooner in the southern states.

Turning off Main Street, Hannah drove past a varied collection of homes: two-story Victorians, a red-brick colonial with gleaming white columns, quaint craftsman cottages, cozy bungalows, and one-story brick homes.

Mama D would approve. The whole town looked clean and well-maintained, as if people took pride in their community.

Hannah returned to Main Street and parked in front of the Hotel de Crawdad. Would it be too expensive? She did have money, but she needed to be careful and use it wisely.

The available furnished duplex was still an option. But renting something long-term didn't make sense until Hannah was sure this was where she wanted to stay.

She groaned as she glanced over her shoulder at her belongings. How was she supposed to get her belongings into a nice hotel? What would they think if they saw her walking through the lobby, carrying plastic grocery bags and her clothes wrapped in a bedspread and bed sheets?

At least she had one suitcase with a makeup bag, a change of clothes, and the items from Francesca's safe deposit box. Hannah nibbled on her bottom lip. Maybe she could sneak in the rest of her belongings late at night, or just lock the car and hope for the best. It wasn't like she wore designer clothes or expensive jewelry.

Hannah fingered the gold chain around her neck that Francesca had given her for her eighteenth birthday. Supposedly, it came from Paris. Hannah wore the chain and the small gold hoop earrings that Mama D gave her. Those items were the ones Hannah cherished the most. Everything else in the car was replaceable.

After an easy hotel check-in, Hannah moved her car into the back lot, where the check-in lady promised it would be safe.

Hannah dragged her suitcase into her room and locked the door behind her.

The room contained two queen-size beds, a desk, and a chair. The bathroom featured a claw-foot tub and shower. Exposed beams were on the ceiling, a brick wall, and a balcony that overlooked Main Street. She couldn't believe the room's price wasn't higher.

Sitting at the desk in her room, Hannah opened her laptop. Crawdad Beach would be home base to maybe, once and for all, discover the truth about Francesca. Plus, where Mama D now lived and the town where Francesca and Hannah were born were both within easy driving distance.

Now it was time to get to work. On her laptop, Hannah entered the town and the names of Francesca's parents from her birth certificate into the online search to find people and their addresses. If the couple were really dead, maybe Hannah could find an obituary. If they were alive, maybe, just maybe, she had grandparents who would want to see her.

A listing of people and addresses filled her screen. Fifteen men with the same name lived in that town, but only one man's listing showed a wife with the same name as the one on Francesca's birth certificate.

The hair on the back of Hannah's neck raised.

Were Francesca's parents still alive? Did Hannah have living grandparents?

Chapter 9

The amount of information online was creepy. Was it only a coincidence that the people had the same names as Francesca's parents?

Hannah brought up the map program on the internet and typed in the address. She could get there in forty-five minutes. It was too late now. Tomorrow, she'd meet Mama D's cousin, Gloria Carter, then talk to Wanda King about the new job. After that, Hannah could drive over to the town and try to find out if they were Francesca's parents.

Hoping to get a good night's sleep, Hannah got ready for bed and pulled the soft covers around her. If Francesca's parents weren't dead, that would mean Hannah might have living grandparents. What would that be like? She smiled at the thought of being surrounded by big, happy hugs.

Then again, what if Francesca said they were dead because they were horrible people? What if Hannah found them and they wanted nothing to do with her?

How many lies had Francesca told her? And what was the deal with Johan Rauchmann? Was he her father? Did he get rid of Francesca, or was the car wreck merely a terrible accident?

Hannah moaned. What if she never found out the truth?

What if coming to Crawdad Beach was a mistake?

She should have gone with Mama D to live. What if she didn't like the people at the beauty shop? What if they didn't like her? What if she didn't make any friends?

Hannah swatted at the what-ifs buzzing around her mind. When she was a little girl, Mama D taught her to pray about the things that bothered her. Not only to pray, but to visualize God's loving hands taking her worries and problems and holding them close to His heart while she slept. When Hannah did that, she always had a great night's sleep, and when she would wake up, her worries seemed to have gone away or were much more manageable.

She sighed and began praying, talking to God about all the things that worried her. Hannah cringed. Shouldn't she feel guilty for bringing all her problems to God? Didn't He have enough to handle with all the evil and craziness of the world? Then again, even God's Son, Jesus, prayed and told us to pray because God cares for us and loves us. The thought felt like a comforting hug. Rolling over, she closed her eyes.

The next morning, a warm, gentle breeze played through Hannah's long hair as she walked through the downtown area. Birds chirped in the trees, and puffy white clouds drifted in the brilliant blue sky. What a difference a good night's sleep made.

The concerns about Francesca and Johan, and wondering if Francesca's parents were alive, Hannah's new job, the move to Crawdad Beach, and finding new friends hadn't vanished entirely, yet a quiet contentment and peace filled her.

Admiring the cute town, Hannah strolled along the sidewalk. Most of the buildings' second-floor balconies were a fragrant profusion of flowers.

A white-haired couple walking a little white dog said hello as they passed by. A young woman smiled as she pushed a stroller.

Hannah went by Rolling in the Dough Bakery. A middle-aged couple emerged from the building. The aroma of freshly baked bread, cinnamon, sugary glaze, and rich butter enveloped her in the scent of deliciousness. She'd already eaten a protein bar, but it didn't come close to the tantalizing smells coming from the bakery.

Stopping in front of Knick Knack's Antique Store, Hannah peeked in the shop window. From what she could see, the old building held all sorts of interesting-looking items, from furniture to books, old toys, and—she grinned to herself—all kinds of knick-knacks.

Mama D would love this place. Hannah snapped a few photos with her phone, then continued her journey.

Despite being nervous about meeting Mama D's cousin, Hannah chuckled at Doohickeys Store's sign, boasting that they carried a wide variety of hardware, building supplies, and any "whatchamacallit" needed.

As Hannah entered the building, the old wooden floors creaked in greeting. The ceiling's tin looked original, with a unique patina from years of use. Neat, dust-free, dark wooden shelves displayed a fascinating mix of old and new items.

Cutting and styling hair, she understood. Home repair projects, not so much.

"Can I help you?" A neatly trimmed, brown-haired guy with brown eyes, maybe a little older than she was, walked toward her.

Hannah nodded. "Yes, I'm looking for Gloria Carter."

A wide smile stretched across his face. "I'm Sammie Banks. Follow me." He glanced over his shoulder. "I haven't seen you before. Are you new in town?"

"Yes. I got here yesterday."

"Great. Welcome to Crawdad Beach." He led her to the back of the building, past a large display on the wall of old farming utensils. He tapped on the frame of the door leading to an office. "Gloria. Someone is here to see you."

"Thank you, Sammie."

Hannah peeked in as a middle-aged woman with a beautiful milk chocolate complexion and sparkling brown eyes rose from her desk chair. "Hannah Joy!" She rushed over and enveloped Hannah in a big hug. "I couldn't wait to meet Dorthea's Goddaughter in person."

Stepping back, Gloria took Hannah's hands in hers. "Dorthea has been sending me photos of you since you were just a baby. I've been praying for you for years."

Tears welled in Hannah's eyes, stinging and blurring her vision. Mama D sent photos, and Ms. Carter had been praying for her? How sweet.

Gloria's eyes crinkled at the corners with her grin. "Little girl, you've had more prayers going up for you than you can imagine."

After a wonderful time visiting Gloria, Hannah stepped out of the building and onto Main Street's sidewalk. Gloria reminded Hannah of Mama D as laughter filled the air, and time flew by.

Hannah turned her attention to the town around her. For a small city, it sure stayed busy. Most of the parking spaces in front of the buildings were occupied, leaving only a few empty. A group of middle-aged women, their voices excitedly talking about Knick Knacks and a found treasure, hurried past.

Two older gentlemen walking a small black and white dog stopped in front of her.

The one holding the dog's leash smiled. "You must be Hannah Joy. I'm Henry Doss. Welcome to Crawdad Beach."

Hannah took a step back. How did he know her

name?

"Please forgive my forwardness." Mr. Doss's bright blue eyes crinkled in the corners with his gentle smile. "We heard you were moving to town. Good news travels fast in our community."

"I'm your back-door neighbor. Chester Taylor," the other man said. "You'll probably meet my wife, Maybelline, at the beauty shop or if you visit the library."

Hannah's fingers curled into her palm as she debated whether she should run screaming, *stranger danger*, worry that the town was filled with gossips, or feel grateful that her move here was considered good news.

The little dog leaned against her leg as though providing comfort.

"That's Filbert," Mr. Doss said. "He possesses an uncanny ability to discern the goodness in others."

Hannah leaned down and rubbed the little dog's furry head. "Thank you, Filbert."

The pup responded with tail wags.

"We're heading to Tiddlywinks Restaurant for breakfast if you'd like to join us," Chester Taylor said.

"Thank you, Mr. Taylor, for the invitation. I've already eaten and need to get to the Beauty Shop."

"Call me Chester. I'm not into formal stuff. My body might be older, but inside I'm still twenty-five." He stood ramrod straight, as if he were a military man.

A low chuckle rumbled in Mr. Doss's chest. "That

explains a lot."

"Now, Henry," Chester said with a mischievous grin, "you've been known to get into a little trouble yourself."

Mr. Doss's eyes twinkled as he raised an eyebrow. "Most of those situations came when we were together."

"True." Chester nudged his friend. "But you've got to admit we had fun."

Mr. Doss chuckled, then turned his attention to Hannah. "It was nice to meet you."

Chester smiled. "Good to meet you, Hannah. We hope you enjoy living here."

"Thank you. Nice to meet you both, too." The sounds of their playful banter faded into the distance as the two men walked toward the restaurant.

Between the warm welcome from Gloria Carter and the two older men, maybe Hannah didn't need to be worried about finding friends after all.

She stopped in front of the Curl and Dye Beauty Shop, straightened her shoulders, and opened the door.

A little bell over the door announced her arrival. The whirring of hair dryers, the scent of hairspray, the murmur of conversations, and bursts of laughter filled the air.

Hannah recognized Wanda King's short, blonde hair styled in a textured, layered look as she hurried toward her.

"Hannah Joy, it's so good to see you in person. You're even cuter than on our Zoom call." A warm hug enveloped

Hannah before she could react.

Wanda stepped out of the embrace and smiled. "Welcome to Crawdad Beach and Curl and Dye." Blue eyeshadow and pink lipstick accentuated her pretty face.

Hannah instantly liked the woman. "Nice to meet you, Ms. King."

Her new boss waved a dismissive hand. "Call me Wanda." She turned toward the others in the beauty shop. "Ladies, this is Hannah Joy. She'll be starting work here tomorrow morning. Please give her a big Curl and Dye welcome."

The other two stylists held up their hair dryers as though in a salute and yelled, "Welcome!"

The sudden attention sent heat to Hannah's cheeks, but she gave them a smile. "Thank you so much."

Wanda took Hannah's hand and led her to the empty station. "This will be your new place," Wanda said with a proud smile. "Everything should be ready for you."

"Thank you. But I don't have my own scissors." Hannah looked away. Her Pittsburgh coworkers bragged about owning their own equipment.

Her boss opened the top drawer. "No worries. I've taken care of all that. I want the best for my employees."

Hannah calculated the cost. "Will using the tools come out of my paycheck?" Her last employer charged her an extra fifty dollars a month.

"No," Wanda's head tilted. "They're part of your

station, just like the chair, mirror, and the use of anything in the facility."

"Really?" Hannah grinned. "Thank you. That's nice of you."

"Of course. I want you to be successful. It's good business for us all. Now, let me introduce you to the other stylists." Wanda pointed toward a pleasingly plump middle-aged woman with shoulder-length brown hair. "This is Alma."

The smiling woman paused her scissors. "Nice to meet you, Hannah. We're glad you're here."

"Thank you. Nice to meet you, too."

"Next is Daphne." Wanda led Hannah to a thin, middle-aged, spiky-haired redhead.

The redhead grinned and turned off her hairdryer. "Welcome to Curl and Dye, Hannah. Hope you love it here." Daphne turned back to her client and pooched out her stomach. "I told the doctor I had a tumor because my belly got so big. It turned out I had simply gained weight." Daphne chuckled. "Who knew eating a bag of potato chips every day would do that?"

The older lady in the chair grinned. "Were they the small bags like you put in a kid's lunch, or the family size?"

"Well. Okay, so it was family size. But, since I live alone, I'm a family. Just one bag a day for me."

Wanda chuckled and touched Hannah's arm. "Come on to my office, and we'll chat for a few minutes. I'm sure you're still busy getting settled." She led Hannah to a small, tidy office at the back of the building.

Hannah perched on the edge of a plush, comfortable chair opposite a beautiful, light gray desk with elegant gold accents. Behind the desk, a matching bookshelf displayed a colorful array of hairstyling books and a variety of framed photos of Wanda with what appeared to be her grown children. Hannah averted her eyes. Had Francesca cared enough to show her picture to anyone?

Opening her top desk drawer, Wanda took out and opened a folder. She explained the shop to Hannah, detailing her stylist's responsibilities, reviewing the salary and commissions, vacation and personal time policies, and outlining how to handle any difficulties that might arise.

"I emailed you your schedule." Wanda continued. "Most of the people in town already have a stylist they prefer. However, since Celeste retired, you'll pick up most of her clients. Do you have any questions for me?"

Hannah hoped she remembered everything that Wanda had said. "I don't have questions right now. Since the shop opens at eight, should I be here at seven-thirty to get set up?"

"That would work well on your first day. After that, just arrive whenever you need to get ready for your clients. Tomorrow morning, your first customer is scheduled for 8:15. If you have a customer who needs an early or late appointment, I'm flexible. I have an apartment over the shop, so I'm here most of the time." Wanda slid a business card toward her and then stood. "Call my cell if you ever need anything."

Hannah rose to her feet. "Thank you for giving me this opportunity."

"My pleasure. I know you'll do great."

Hoping that was true, Hannah said goodbye to everyone. She stepped outside and checked her schedule. Tomorrow, she had six clients scheduled—five women and one man. All but the guy had been Celeste's customers.

Hannah stared at the sky and silently prayed for help. She just had to make this work. Failure was not an option.

She picked up her pace. Next stop, she'd drive to the other town and see if she could find Francesca's parents.

Chapter 10

"4201 Packard. This is the place."

Hannah stopped her car across the street from the one-story brick home. Her heart rapped against her chest as if knocking on the door to the house.

She licked her lips but ended up biting her lower lip. A bad habit she'd had since childhood, but thought she'd conquered years ago.

Did she want to dig into the past? Could this be where Francesca's parents once lived or still live? The place her mother never even let her know about.

Flowers filled the well-groomed landscaping. A tall, white vertical sign stood on the porch, the word "Welcome" painted in a bright teal color. A fabric yard sign near the front door flapped in the breeze with the words, "As for me and my house, we will serve the Lord."

Hannah shook her head. Francesca couldn't have grown up in a welcoming place like this. Not with her negative view of God. Why had she been that way? Was it because she had mean parents, or because Francesca had been in love with a married man? Maybe her frustration with God had stemmed from her own anger and regret.

Leaning back in her seat, Hannah gazed at the photo she'd brought of Francesca when she was younger. She stood with a couple who could have been her parents. Francesca looked so happy, like she didn't have a care in the world.

Hannah swallowed her tightening throat. "What happened to you, Francesca?"

For as long as she could remember, her mother had looked worried, her smile never quite reaching her eyes. Each visit had been short and rushed, like she had to be somewhere else and didn't want to be there.

That hadn't bothered Hannah that much, not until she discovered the truth that Francesca was really her mother. Each visit after that only deepened Hannah's ache, a constant reminder of her mother's rejection and the pain of not belonging.

Hot tears pricked Hannah's eyes, and she squeezed them shut, trying to stem the flow. *God, what is the truth? Why didn't she want me?*

A thought struck Hannah with the force of a physical blow, leaving her breathless and disoriented. Maybe something else, something more, was going on with Francesca's visits.

Maybe she'd been afraid.

Francesca could have been fearful of her parents, Johan, or someone else. She might have hidden Hannah at Mama D's to protect her from Johan.

Hannah turned her attention back to the house. Was the pretty façade only a disguise to conceal evil and cruel people? A chill went down her spine.

Her dream was to have a loving mother and father, but reality might have been a nightmare of a flawed or even dangerous couple that considered her an unwanted burden to be discarded.

Mama D often told Hannah to leave yesterday alone, but Hannah couldn't deny the part of her that wanted answers.

A shiny red SUV sat in the driveway, so someone might be home. Hannah groaned. Did she really want to knock on the door? What would she say?

Hi, sorry to bother you, but do you know Francesca?

Hello, my name is Hannah Joy. Prepare to meet your granddaughter.

She could hold up the photo and ask the homeowners if they recognized the people in the picture. Or she could pretend to be selling something to get a glimpse of who lived there.

No, she didn't want to be dishonest and lie like Francesca.

Wondering about everything wasn't solving anything. Clutching the photo in her hand, Hannah opened her car door. She'd show the picture to whoever answered and then ask if they knew who the people were.

Hannah stood as she second-guessed herself. Her

breath caught in her throat. Maybe she shouldn't be here. What if Francesca's parents knew she'd been born but wanted nothing to do with an illegitimate child?

Who would want a granddaughter from an illicit affair? Why else wouldn't they try to find her?

Hannah steadied her expression and pulled back her shoulders. She wanted to know, needed to know the truth, at least some nugget of truth about who she really was.

She'd master her feelings again, lock them away in the steel vault, and throw away the key. She could do this.

With a squeak, the house's front door opened, and a little girl with long brown hair skipped down the steps, her bright pink shoes flashing. A young couple followed behind.

"Last one to the car is a rotten egg," the man said.

A squeal of pure joy came from the little girl as she dashed to the SUV and scrambled inside.

The man, woman, and little girl were all smiles as they drove away.

A longing washed over Hannah as she sank back into the worn upholstery of her car. She never had a family like that. She never would.

She shouldn't have gotten her hopes up or thought the worst about the people she'd never met. The young couple could not be her grandparents.

Francesca's parents were probably dead, just like her mother had claimed.

Besides that, the house was perfect, with a perfect yard, perfect landscaping, and perfect welcoming signs.

Hannah didn't belong here. Nothing about her existence was perfect.

Until the end, Francesca denied being her mother, and Hannah's birth certificate listed 'unknown' as her father.

She never belonged anywhere.

Hannah rested her head on the steering wheel. What was she going to do now? She didn't want to go back alone to her hotel room.

The ocean.

She could go there. She'd only seen pictures and videos, but never experienced it herself.

Hannah steered toward the nearby beach. Parking her car, she stepped out and breathed deeply of the salty air. She crossed a boardwalk of sun-bleached wooden planks that led to the beach.

Removing her sandals, Hannah stepped onto the warm sand and wiggled her toes in the soft grains. The beach buzzed with activity; sunbathers relaxed under colorful umbrellas, while the rhythmic thud of volleyballs and joyful shrieks came from those playing in the water.

Seagulls dipped and flew overhead in the gentle wind as Hannah walked along the shoreline. Laughter carried from a family with small children playing in shallow water close to the shoreline.

What would that have been like? To have been in a family with loving parents? Though she cherished Mama D's love and care, an ache remained for a place to truly call home.

A dog chased a stick into the shallows, tail wagging, as its owners cheered from the beach—a portrait of joyful belonging that made Hannah's throat tighten.

Hannah moved to the water's edge and let the cool waves lap over her toes. She'd been foolish to search for family at an unfamiliar doorstep.

Since Francesca was born in South Carolina, her parents might have raised her overseas. The photos could have been taken in France.

There were so many questions that might never be answered.

For a while, Hannah simply stood, letting the ocean air clear her mind.

Other people had their own problems. One look at the news, and it was obvious the world was a mess. Nobody wanted to hear about her problems and questions.

She crossed to a quiet patch of sand near the dunes, sat, and drew her knees up close. The waves rolled against the shore, in and out, their foamy crests whispering secrets to the sand.

Lifting her face to the sky, Hannah sent up silent prayers for help, guidance, comfort, and peace.

A breeze blew through her hair, cooling her warm neck. The ache of not knowing the truth about Francesca, Hannah's birth, her father's identity, and if her grandparents were still living, surprisingly mingled with a gentle hope—a fragile but growing belief that God would create a place for her in this world, even if it looked different from what she'd ever imagined.

Chapter 11

The rhythmic whir of hair dryers, conversations, and snipping scissors faded into the background as Hannah concentrated on incorporating a gentle massage technique while shampooing her client's hair. A peaceful look of bliss rested on the woman's face.

The easy laughter and shared jokes between Wanda, Alma, and Daphne made Hannah feel like she'd known them for years. Even the retired beautician's customers seemed to accept her without issue.

With the final rinse complete, Hannah gently wrapped her client's hair in a thick towel. She then helped the lady into the styling chair and secured a bright pink cape around her neck.

As much as Hannah enjoyed her job, she was never sure what to say to her clients. Making small talk was clumsy and awkward, especially since she didn't know many people in town.

Fortunately, Daphne and Alma spent most of their time chatting, and Hannah's customers seemed to enjoy listening to the other fun conversations.

"Where did you move from?" Her client asked her.

Surprised by the need for a conversation, Hannah froze for a moment. "Pennsylvania."

"Such a long way. Did you move with your family?"

"No, ma'am." Hannah did not want to explain anything about that situation. The relationship with Francesca hadn't been like Hannah wanted, yet God took care of her, and Mama D always loved her. For that, she would always be grateful.

Her client's kind hazel eyes surveyed Hannah. "Well, I hope you like it here."

The shop phone rang, and Wanda answered, then hurried toward Alma. "It's Richard Worthington, the lawyer. He was wondering if you could work him in this afternoon. He wants to look his best for a client meeting."

Alma let out a sigh. "I would love to, but I'm leaving early today."

Wanda snapped her fingers. "That's right. I forgot."

"I'll take him," Daphne hollered.

Alma grinned. "Thanks, friend. I know you'll do a great job."

Hannah couldn't believe it. The toxic atmosphere at her previous workplace had been a cutthroat battle for customers, where backstabbing and underhanded tactics were the standard operating procedure.

After finishing with her client, Hannah cleaned up her station and checked her schedule. A guy named Cameron Doss would be next.

Hannah laid out her scissors and clippers as she waited. Was Cameron related to Henry Doss, the kind older gentleman who owned the cute little black and white dog named Filbert?

The bell over the door announced someone's arrival. Hannah turned to watch a handsome guy with dark brown disheveled hair stop at the front counter.

With a big grin, Wanda led the man toward her. "Hannah Joy, this is Cameron Doss." Wanda wiggled her eyebrows at Hannah.

Embarrassment rocketed heat to her face at Wanda's not-so-subtle message that Cameron was cute and probably single. Hannah did a quick glance at her client. "Nice to meet you."

Cameron's dark-brown-eyed gaze flitted toward her. "You too. Just a trim, please." His jaw clenched as he sat in the chair and focused on the mirror. It didn't look like he was staring at himself; more like he'd zoned out somewhere beyond the shop.

"Would you like me to wash your hair? We have a shampoo for guys that smells amazing."

He remained silent, his gaze fixed elsewhere. "Yeah, sure."

Hannah directed him to the sinks. As he sat, she wrapped a towel around his muscular shoulders. He wasn't an overly big guy, just nicely built. He rested the back of his head against the sink and closed his eyes.

If Cameron was related to Henry, he certainly wasn't as friendly. Hannah tried not to focus on that fact as she shampooed his hair.

As she worked, the tension left his jaw. Hannah gave herself a mental pat on the back. Her massage techniques were effective even on the most hardened customers. She finished, then wrapped Cameron's head in a towel.

His eyes opened, and he stared at her as though seeing her for the first time. "Thanks for the wash." His smile was shy, almost hesitant.

"You're welcome." Hannah led him back to her stylist chair and snapped a black cape around his neck. "You mentioned a trim. I think your hair might need a little more help than that."

He gazed at her through the mirror. "Yeah, you're right. It's been a while since I've had anything done. Just do whatever you think best."

As Hannah assessed how to take care of her client, she stood behind him and ran her hands through his hair. He'd need quite a bit off the sides and top, and the back had a slight cowlick, which would require attention to get it to behave. With a good haircut, he would be even more handsome.

She glanced in the mirror.

One of Cameron's eyebrows raised as his gaze met hers.

Heat rising to her cheeks, Hannah jerked her fingers

out of his hair, grabbed her scissors, and got to work. She shouldn't let her mind drift. She did *not* need a man in her life.

Hannah used the clippers on the back of his neck, shaping up his hairline.

It wasn't like she'd dated very much. She'd gone out with a few guys she had met at church or through the homeschool coop. One she had a serious crush on, but he didn't seem to want anything to do with her.

The beauticians at her last place tried to set her up on dates, but most of the guys they suggested made her skin crawl. Hannah turned them all down. She'd rather live alone.

She could take care of herself.

At least she hoped she could.

Cameron closed his eyes. He shouldn't be staring at the dark-haired beauty with green eyes and magic fingers.

Man, he hadn't been this relaxed in months. Hopefully, he hadn't drooled while Hannah worked. After the shampoo and massage thing she did, she could shave his head, and he wouldn't care.

Maybe he could get in every week for a shampoo, massage, and trim. No matter what Hannah charged, it would be worth it.

Since moving from Texas, Cameron had ignored his hair. He did need to look decent. Stopping in every week wouldn't be a bad thing, and Hannah's scalp massage shampoo would help him relieve tension.

But if he did that, would she think he was some stuck-up guy only interested in how he looked?

Cameron internally groaned. He didn't need to worry about someone he didn't even know.

He did *not* need to be attracted to anyone.

He'd messed up his life enough.

Chapter 12

With a final swipe of her cloth, Hannah finished cleaning her station.

Saturday afternoon at 12:05, and the rest of the day was hers to command. Unfortunately, besides getting some lunch, she wasn't sure what to do.

"Are you ready to check out the duplex apartment I told you about?" Wearing a big smile, Wanda came toward her.

Hannah bit her lip. Was she ready to put down more permanent roots? "Maybe? I'm not sure."

"It's still available, really nice, affordable, and the owners are super people. We love having you here. You're a big part of the team now. Crawdad Beach needs you." Wanda's hopeful expression and kind words were hard to resist.

"Okay." Hannah grinned. "I'll go check it out." As nice as her hotel room was, she was ready to have a place to call her own.

"Yay! You will love it. Do you need help moving in?"

"No, I can handle that. Thank you for the offer, though." Hannah sure didn't want Wanda seeing her belongings bundled in bed sheets. Way too embarrassing.

"I'll let Julie know you're coming." Wanda's painted nails clicked a staccato rhythm against her phone as she tapped out a text. "Dustin and Julie Bowman are the owners and live in the duplex next door."

Hannah didn't want to disappoint her boss, but there were so many unknowns. "What if I don't like it? I mean, I'm sure I will, but what if I don't?" Hoping she didn't disappoint her boss, Hannah retrieved her purse from the bottom drawer.

"You'll love it. I promise. But if you don't, the loft apartments here on Main Street are also nice. Follow me to the office and let me get you your first paycheck."

Hannah caught up with her boss. "You're already paying me?" At her previous job, she was paid only once a month.

"Sure. It's more paperwork, but I want everyone to enjoy working here. Happy employees make happy customers." Wanda stopped at her desk and handed Hannah her first paycheck from Curl and Dye. "Do you have a bank already? If not, I have cash in the safe."

"I'll be okay. I have an account with the bank that has an ATM in town. I can make a deposit there."

"Perfect. Then, I'll let you get on your way. Oh, do you need lunch? I have some chicken salad upstairs I can wrap up for you to take."

Hannah grinned. "I'll be fine. Thank you. You don't

have to do that for me." Between Wanda supplying lunches and enjoying home-cooked dinners at Gloria's house, Hannah was being spoiled rotten and had probably gained a few pounds.

"I enjoy making extra food since I miss my kiddos," Wanda said as she walked with Hannah toward the front door. "They're both living on their own in other states, and besides that, it's no fun to cook for just one person."

Hannah stopped with her hand on the doorknob and turned toward her boss. "Thank you for making me feel so welcome."

"Of course." Wanda pulled her close for a long, tight hug. "Thank you for being here."

Surprised by the affection and that she was being thanked, Hannah froze for a second before hugging her boss back.

Emotions swelled in her throat along with a tingling behind her eyes. Embarrassed that she was about to cry, Hannah stepped back. "I'll see you Monday morning."

With the all-too-familiar ache welling in her chest, she hurried out of the beauty shop. Francesca never wanted to be her mother, didn't even let Hannah live with her, and never even cared enough to tell her the truth face-to-face that she was her mother.

Hannah stomped her way down the sidewalk. Forget a home-cooked meal or being tucked into bed at night by a loving mother. Francesca gave birth, then sent Hannah to live elsewhere, only visiting when it suited her schedule as she traveled the globe with her lover.

Hannah groaned. She had to quit thinking like that. Nobody wanted to come to a pity party. She shoved the negative emotion to the back of her mind, focusing on the present.

The past couldn't be changed. Nothing could fix what had happened or hadn't happened. The truth was, Mama D loved her and always would, and their family was wonderful to Hannah. They were her true family.

Hannah pulled back her shoulders as she walked to where she'd left her car. She needed to stand on her own two feet. She'd check out the duplex apartment and make sure that would be where she wanted to stay.

She drove through the peaceful streets until she found the correct address. Hannah stopped at the end of a cul-de-sac in front of a sea-green duplex. A white door, window shutters, and garage gave it a crisp, clean look. Flowerbeds bursting with color surrounded the neatly trimmed lawn.

As much as she enjoyed eating at the bakery in the mornings, she missed being able to fix what she wanted. Mama D had taught her to cook delicious meals, sew intricate patterns, cultivate a thriving garden, and with other skills that helped her take care of herself.

Yep, she could adult with the best of them.

Hannah grabbed her purse, walked to the right-side

duplex where the owners lived, and knocked on the door.

A few minutes passed before it opened, revealing a woman with warm, inviting brown eyes and shoulder-length sandy brown hair. "You must be Hannah Joy. I'm Julie Bowman. Wanda said you were coming. I've already got the key." Julie turned her head. "Dustin, I'll be right back."

She motioned for Hannah to follow. "The apartment is fully furnished and ready for you to move right in." Julie handed the key.

As she stepped inside, Hannah tried not to let her jaw drop. The living room had a white couch, two floral chairs, a coffee table, and a flat-screen TV on a white cabinet. Light blue paint covered the walls, and a wood-look vinyl was on the floor.

The rear of the open floor plan room featured a kitchen with white cabinets and a dining area, complete with a round, whitewashed wooden table and four chairs. Glass French doors at the back led to a screened-in porch.

"Are you enjoying working at Curl and Dye?" Julie asked.

"Yes," Hannah nodded. "It's been nice working there and meeting new people."

"Crawdad Beach is a wonderful place. By the way, the kitchen includes plates, silverware, cooking utensils, and there's a laundry room with a washer and dryer."

"That's great. Thank you." Hannah couldn't believe

how nice everything looked, and the place even smelled new.

"Let me show you the bedroom." Julie motioned for her to follow. "The bed is ready with clean sheets. If you need a cover, there's a spare at the top of the closet."

Hannah entered the peaceful-feeling room. White shutter shades covered the windows, and a light teal bedspread and rattan furniture decorated the room. The bathroom shower curtain depicted a cute beach scene.

There had to be a mistake. The place was too nice for such low rent. Hannah stared at the key in her hand. "Ms. Bowman, this duplex is very nice. Wanda King quoted me a price, but that figure seems way too low."

"I gave the quote to Wanda, so I'm sure it's correct."

"Really? I didn't think I'd ever be able to afford something this nice." Heat rocketed to Hannah's face. She didn't mean to say that out loud. What was she thinking? She had money now. She could afford the place even at a higher price.

A gentle smile played on Julie's lips. "Hannah, my husband is the town's mayor and owns a software security firm, and I'm a lawyer. We consider this duplex part of our ministry to help those who come to our town. We pray for each of our tenants."

"You prayed for me?" Hannah's vision blurred at the sweet thought. Why did she keep getting so emotional?

"Of course, you're a long way from home, so don't

hesitate to contact me or my husband if you need anything. Our phone numbers and information about the security system, cable, and Wi-Fi are on the counter."

Julie took a piece of paper and a pen out of one of the kitchen drawers and handed them to her. "Here's the rental agreement. Just sign at the bottom and move on in."

Hannah composed herself as she stared at the one-page rental agreement. That was all there was to it?

Her last ratty apartment had a ten-page document outlining practically anything that might happen to the property. If she left even a nail hole in a wall, they charged extra. And boy, did they hit her with a hefty bill for leaving her furniture and not cleaning the apartment before she left.

Why was Julie so trusting? She seemed harmless enough, but why would people with well-paying jobs live in a duplex and rent out the other one?

Hannah wasn't getting any weird vibes from the situation, plus Wanda must trust her, but Hannah still sent up a quick, silent prayer for protection.

She carefully read through the agreement. The duplex apartment's surprisingly low cost meant she could add to her savings account each month. Hannah signed her name as a tenant.

"Great," Julie smiled. "I'll get you a copy. Do you need help moving in?"

"No, I'll be fine." She did not want anyone to see her

belongings were still in sheets, a bedspread, and plastic grocery bags.

"If you need anything at all, please don't hesitate to call or stop by; we're always happy to help." Julie moved to the door. "By the way, Chester and Maybelline Taylor's house is behind the duplex. They're a sweet, older couple who've lived in the area for over fifty years. I'll have to introduce you once you get settled."

Hannah grinned at the memory of meeting Chester and Henry Doss. "I've met Chester."

Julie chuckled. "Why am I not surprised? He does get around town. He's such a nice man, but he's a little mischievous."

After her landlady left, Hannah retrieved her belongings from the car, put her clean clothes away, and took the rest to the washing machine.

Once finished, she took photos with her phone to send to the woman whose love had always been unwavering, trustworthy, and kind. Mama D would be thrilled about Hannah's new place.

Everything was falling into place. She enjoyed working and meeting the people who lived in town. It was as if a weight had fallen off her shoulders.

She had her future in front of her.

Hannah's cell phone pinged. Mama D was probably sending all kinds of hearts about the photos.

Instead, the message read:

Hannah baby, you need to come see me as soon as you can. Come today! I have something I need to show you.

Chapter 13

"**W**hy did she send the letter through you?" Hannah stared at the crisp, creamy-colored envelope.

Mama D's warm, comforting hand rested on Hannah's arm. "Baby, Francesca wanted me to be here when you read what she wrote. She placed the envelope inside the letter she sent me."

"That bad, huh?"

"I believe it will help you understand your mother and her actions."

"Will I need smelling salts or a punching bag?"

Mama D gave a soft chuckle. "You'll be okay. I'm here. One other thing. Francesca's letter was postmarked two days before she died."

Hannah sucked in a breath. "Oh, that's so sad."

Her fingers trembled as she read the two-page letter written in Francesca's elegant handwriting.

My sweet daughter,

I'm so sorry I'm not telling you all of this in person. For my safety and yours, I'm leaving the country.

Please bear with me while I try to explain.

My wonderful parents raised me in a Christian home, but I wanted more out of life. I longed to travel the world and to be somebody. I spent my last two high school years as an exchange student in France. I then received a business degree in Paris and interned at Rauchmann Industries. That is where I met Johan Rauchmann.

Returning to the States, I worked at the company's U.S. headquarters as Johan's personal assistant. He provided me with a townhouse, a luxury sports car, and even a credit card for all my needs. I thought life was wonderful. But before I knew it, everything spiraled out of control, or more accurately, my life fell under Johan's control.

When I became pregnant, Johan was furious. He never wanted another child and demanded that I have an abortion. I told him I couldn't. Placing the baby for adoption was contingent upon his name never being associated with the child's fatherhood.

Before the pregnancy became obvious, I made the excuse that my parents were ill and needed care. I stayed in South Carolina until you were born.

I showed Johan your birth photo. He broke my arm.

A red haze of anger clouded Hannah's vision as she

gripped the paper. "Johan broke her arm?!"

Mama D's eyes, filled with a deep sadness, nodded slowly; a single tear traced a path down her weathered cheek. "Yes. Francesca sometimes had unexplained bruises on her arms—some dark and angry, others barely visible."

Words Mama D would disapprove of ran through Hannah's mind. She growled, her eyes burning with anger as she stared at the words on the letter.

The first year, I flew back and forth to see you at my parents' place. But Johan became suspicious. I knew if he found out that I hadn't put you up for adoption, there would be hell to pay.

I hated being so far away from you. So, I hired Mama D as a full-time in-home caretaker. Mama D agreed because I told her that your father was dead and I traveled too much to keep you at my home.

I know Mama D thought it was a temporary arrangement, but when it continued, she didn't want to lose you. She even offered to adopt you.

I'm so sorry I didn't let her. I know you were happy there. But I was selfish. Selfish in so many ways. I'm so sorry.

Hannah jerked her attention to Mama D. "You wanted

to adopt me?"

"Yes, baby. More than you will ever know."

With a sob caught in her throat, Hannah flung her arms around the precious woman she would always consider her true mom.

Mama D held her tight, the warmth of her embrace a comfort against the tears that shook them both. "You may not be my daughter by birth, but you are my daughter given by God."

Hannah lost it again. Tears streamed down her face as she wept for Francesca and the terrible consequences of her decisions. Hannah mourned the absent relationship with her mother, her cries laced with relief and thankfulness for the love she found in Mama D.

Hannah's lip trembled. "Thank you for always being there for me."

Mama D kissed Hannah's forehead. "Baby, you have always been a blessing to me and my family. You may not have our surname, but you have our hearts."

"Aw, you are so sweet." Wiping her tears, Hannah tried to compose herself so she could read the rest of her mother's letter.

Please forgive me, Hannah. I've asked God, Mama D, and other people I've hurt for forgiveness.

I don't deserve your forgiveness, and I know I can't make up to you for all the years we didn't have together as mother and daughter.

If you hate me, I understand.

Once I've settled somewhere safe, if you'd like to spend time with me, I would love to see you. Please, please be careful.

I have always loved you and will always love you.

Your mother, Francesca

Chapter 14

Her eyes blurry with tears, Hannah stepped away from Mama D's embrace and opened her car door.

They'd stayed up late last night crying and discussing Francesca's letter and wondering if her death was truly an accident. Mama D had even taken the time to explain what she thought and believed during that time. Mama D hadn't realized everything that was going on, but she had known enough to be concerned about Hannah and Francesca's welfare.

Mama D placed her soft, warm hand on Hannah's cheek. "Be safe driving back to Crawdad Beach. Please text or call when you arrive. I'll keep praying. God's got you, baby. He will never leave nor forsake you."

Hannah's throat too tight to speak, she nodded and slid into the driver's seat while keeping her door open.

"I love you, baby," Mama D continued. "Everything's going to be okay. Remember, all things work for the good for those who love God and are called according to His purpose. I know God has a wonderful purpose for your life."

"I love you, too. Thank you for always being there for

me."

With tears in her eyes, Mama D smiled. "God delivering you to my doorstep was, and continues to be, a wonderful blessing. Now, embrace whatever God has planned for your life. As Oswald Chambers said, let the past sleep on the bosom of Christ and leave the irreparable past in His hands, and step out into the irresistible future with Him."

"Irresistible future sounds nice." A flicker of hope grew within Hannah. "Do you really think God has something good planned for me like that?"

"I have no doubt, baby. No doubt at all."

Hannah gave her a wobbly grin. "Leaving the past behind, I press on."

"That's right, sweet one. God knows the plans He has for you to give you a future and a hope."

After closing her car door, Hannah blew a kiss and drove away.

Two hours later, Hannah slumped on a bench under the massive oak tree in the Crawdad Beach community park. The afternoon sun filtered through the branches and leaves, casting shadows on the surrounding area.

Sitting under the big oak reminded her of the tall trees in Mama D's Pennsylvania backyard. Even during storms, the treetops swayed and moved with the wind, yet their roots, deeply embedded in the earth, remained still.

Mama D often reminded Hannah, "Keep your roots

deep in God and His Son, Jesus Christ, then when the storms blow, you can stand firm."

Hannah whimpered. She didn't feel like she was standing firm. Not anymore. It was much easier to be full of faith when she was with Mama D, but on her own, Hannah's faith felt wobbly.

Knowing more of the truth about Francesca and that Johan was an abusive jerk wasn't exactly comforting. Hannah sighed. She needed to stop dwelling on things that couldn't be changed. Of course, that was easier said than done. So much for leaving the past behind and pressing on.

A cheerful whistle of a tune that sounded like an old hymn drifted through the breeze, catching her attention. Hannah got to her feet and walked toward the sound.

Wearing a t-shirt and shorts, Cameron, his back to her, stood knee-deep in the shallow river, his face upturned as though whistling to God in heaven.

Mesmerized, she stood watching. He seemed so at peace. She should have been praising God instead of moaning or being worried about her past.

As she listened, his soothing whistle washed over her, and the weight of her worries seemed to physically lift, leaving her feeling relaxed and refreshed.

When Cameron's tune changed to another, Hannah quietly backed away.

Her foot caught.

With a yelp, Hannah landed hard on her backside.

Cameron's attention jerked toward her. Water splashed as he hurried her way. "Are you okay?"

Embarrassed, Hannah struggled to get to her feet. "Yes, I'm sorry. I didn't mean to interrupt."

He steadied her against him. "I should be the one to apologize. It looks like you tripped over my shoes."

Hannah hadn't even noticed his sneakers lying on the ground. The warmth of his gentle touch on her skin, she self-consciously dusted off the back of her sundress. Finished, she stole a glance in his direction.

Cameron was smiling at her. He cleared his throat and stepped back. "I'm sorry my shoes snuck up on your foot."

"I guess they're called sneakers for a reason." Hannah bit her lip. She couldn't believe she was actually trying to joke with someone of the male persuasion.

He chuckled. "Good one. Are you sure you're okay?"

"I'm fine. Again, I'm sorry to interrupt."

A red hue crept up his neck as his gaze moved from her to the ground. "I didn't know anyone was around." He grabbed his shoes and slipped his feet inside.

"You have a nice whistle."

"Thanks. I can't sing, so I whistle."

"Must make it hard during a church service."

Cameron grinned as he stood next to her. "True. I've learned to mouth the words in public. Much safer for those within earshot." His dark-brown-eyed gaze held hers for a moment. "You want to take a walk with me?"

She gave him a grin as excitement and curiosity fluttered in her stomach. "Yes, that sounds nice."

Cameron pretended to watch where he was going, but he kept sneaking glances at Hannah. Despite the burning embarrassment of being caught whistling, the unexpected encounter made it worthwhile.

He hated that she'd tripped on his shoes, but she handled it so well that it made her even more attractive. Hannah looked close to his age, probably younger, with a hint of shyness and innocence.

Not that he was looking to date anyone. Nope. Not going to go there again.

However, having a female friend would be nice. "South Carolina is a long way from Pennsylvania. What brought you to Crawdad Beach?"

Hannah's gaze flicked his way, her eyes lingering for a fleeting second before she looked away. "I wanted to be close to where a friend lived, and a job was available. How about you?"

"I have family here. An aunt offered me a job to work at her building and renovating company." He would not explain the real reason he moved here—no sense airing dirty laundry when it still stunk like dirty socks.

"Do you enjoy your work?" Hannah asked.

"Yeah, I do," Cameron said. "It's incredibly satisfying to renovate and build something and see immediate results. How about you? Do you enjoy working at the beauty shop?"

"Yes." Hannah nodded, a slight smile playing on her lips. "I love being able to cut and style hair."

"You do a great job. Plus, the massage shampoo thing you do is incredible." He wiggled his fingers.

A mischievous glint danced in her eyes. "I've been working on my technique."

"Any time you want to practice, call me."

A bird twilled in a tree branch overhead as they continued their walk.

Cameron turned toward her. "So, I've been wondering how often I could come in for a shampoo and cut without you thinking I was some snobby guy that only cared about my looks."

Hannah's eyes seemed to dance with pleasure. "I wouldn't think that, and I wouldn't mind if you wanted a shampoo and cut every week."

Cameron's smile widened. "I'll call and make a standing appointment."

Chapter 15

With the roof finished, the interior work on the house was moving right along. Cameron whistled while hanging drywall in the hall bathroom.

As embarrassed as he was that Hannah had caught him yesterday afternoon, whistling away with his feet submerged in the river. Seeing her again had made it worthwhile. Besides being beautiful, her cute sense of humor made her even more attractive.

Hannah's presence had been great, but the Sunday morning sermon had been even better—it gave him a whole new perspective. He couldn't change what had happened with Ivy and the lies she'd told, but God knew the truth.

He knew he needed to leave it all in God's hands. The bitterness and unforgiveness had festered within him, a silent, self-inflicted wound that only hurt himself.

Yesterday, he had prayed and given that mess to God, forgiving Ivy for all she'd done and said. As a result, he was free. Ivy would still have to answer to God for the things she'd done.

Katherine came into the room. "Sorry, I was gone this

morning. Had another incident with the homeowner over on Chestnut Street."

Curious, Cameron stopped and glanced at his aunt. "What happened this time?"

Katherine gave a slow shake of her head. "We'd already finished the drywall in his new bathroom when he decided he wanted a medicine cabinet. So, instead of waiting for us, he took a hammer to the wall and destroyed a four-foot section. Unfortunately, he'd demolished the wrong wall."

He raised his eyebrows. "I thought the plumbing was already installed."

"It was."

"So, he didn't stop to think the pipes sticking out of the floor would be where the sink would be?"

Katherine chuckled. "I guess not. Bless his heart, he means well. He just can't seem to understand he should leave it to the professionals."

"Maybe you could post one of us on guard duty until the project's completed. Or you could start filming the crazy things he does to send to one of those television shows where people with no skills wreck their houses."

"Good ideas, but I think we'll just keep working with him. Hopefully, the job will be finished soon. But he mentioned he might want to renovate his kitchen."

Cameron whistled the tune from the movie Jaws.

With a mischievous glint in her eyes, Katherine

grinned. "You know. I'm thinking maybe that would be a project you could handle."

Cameron raised his hands and stepped back. "Please don't do me any favors."

Katherine rubbed her hands together and gave him an evil laugh.

Cameron chuckled as she walked away. He ran from his Texas problems to Crawdad Beach, but maybe God had given him more than he imagined. Coming to this small town and forgiving Ivy brought him a sense of freedom he hadn't known was possible.

Whistling the tune of Amazing Grace, he got back to work.

Hannah fingered the baby-fine silver hair of her customer.

The woman's brown eyes looked at her through the mirror. "I hope you can do something with it. My husband and I are staying at the Hotel de Crawdad for a few days, and after our road trip, my hair just fell flat."

"I'm sure I can get you fixed up. Would you like a shampoo first?"

"Better take her up on that," Daphne said from the next station. "Hannah has customers lined up to experience her magic fingers."

"I could use a shampoo," her smiling client said.

Hannah grinned as she showed the lady to the shampoo sinks at the back. It was funny how many people had called this week for appointments.

She glanced at her next customer waiting in the chairs at the front. The man was almost bald, and he still wanted a shampoo and trim.

The bell dinged as another customer arrived. Henry Doss and Chester Taylor waved at Hannah.

"Got time for us today?" Chester hollered.

Wanda hurried toward them. "Hi, Henry and Chester. Hannah is booked this morning, but one of us might have time."

"No disrespect to you fine ladies," Chester said with a sheepish look, "but well, we were hoping to get a shampoo from Hannah."

Wanda's smile widened. "Ah, so you've heard about Hannah's magic touch, have you?"

Chester's face flushed crimson as his gaze dropped to the floor. "Yeah, maybe."

Even Henry looked like he was blushing. "We don't want to be a bother."

Wanda chuckled as she brought up the scheduling program on her computer. "Hannah has a few openings later today. Will four o'clock work for you both?"

"Yes!" the men said in unison.

After they left, Wanda walked over to Hannah. "Well,

you are getting quite the reputation in town."

"As long as it's a good one," Hannah said.

"Only the best." Wanda gave her a side hug. "You may have to train the rest of us in your massage techniques."

"Sign me up!" Daphne exclaimed.

"Me too!" Alma said as she held up her scissors.

"I'm all in," Wanda said with a big smile. "I'll make dinner one night for the team, and you can show us your magic finger methods."

"Woo hoo!" Daphne said. "We will have customers driving from the surrounding towns."

Hannah grinned as she finished shampooing and massaging her customer's hair. She wrapped her customer's hair in a towel and showed her back to her station.

"You really do have a wonderful talent," her client said, a serene smile playing on her lips.

While working on the lady's hair, Hannah couldn't help but think how lucky she was to be there. She corrected the thought. God had blessed her. Crawdad Beach had turned out to be the perfect place to live and work.

The morning and afternoon zoomed past, and four o'clock was already here. Hannah walked toward where Chester and Henry sat waiting. "Which one of you would like to go first?"

Chester jumped to his feet. "Pick me."

Hannah glanced out front.

A dark gray car with tinted windows cruised slowly past.

Her heart rammed up her throat.

Was that the same car that had been parked outside her apartment building?

Chapter 16

"**A**re you okay? You look like you've seen a ghost."

At Chester's question, Hannah steadied her breathing and pasted on a smile. "I'm fine." Surely it wasn't the same car that had been at her apartment in Pennsylvania. That wouldn't make sense. Maybe it was just one that looked similar.

"You don't look fine to me. What's up? How can we help?"

Henry, his blue eyes wide with concern, came beside her. "We're here for you. Whatever you need."

"It's fine. Really." Hannah looked out the front window again, then back toward the men. "I just thought I saw something."

Henry's gaze met hers. "Do you want me to find out who drove the gray car that passed?"

Surprised he noticed, she shrugged. "I'm sure it wasn't anything."

"Don't you worry. I'll be back soon." He gave her arm a gentle squeeze and then left the building.

Hannah turned her attention back to Chester. "Let's get your hair washed."

Chester hesitated. "Are you sure you're up for this?"

"Of course." Hannah motioned for him to follow her to the sink area. After he sat, she placed a towel around his shoulders, then clipped on a cape.

She wet his hair, squirted on a healthy amount of shampoo, and got to work. It wouldn't make sense if someone had followed her all the way from Pennsylvania. She probably shouldn't have watched that murder mystery last night.

What if that gray car had followed her because of Francesca's death or murder, and the removal of all her belongings? Since Hannah was Francesca and Johan's daughter, no telling what might happen. What would she do?

Chester's hand caught hers. "You might want to slow down a little."

Hannah grimaced. "I'm so sorry." While distracted, she must have gotten a little rough, evidenced by the wide-eyed look on Chester's face.

She slowed her movements, working gently until his eyes closed, and he smiled.

Once she finished, Hannah directed him to her stylist's chair.

"How did you become a beautician?" Chester asked as he sat.

"I've always enjoyed working with hair." She snapped the black cape around his shoulders. "I started out cutting the hair of my dolls, then I started trimming the dog's fur, and then washing and styling Mama D's hair and other people in the neighborhood."

Chester gazed at her in the mirror. "Mama D?"

"She raised me. She's Gloria Carter's cousin."

"Well, then, Mama D must be a sweet woman."

"She is very sweet." Hannah's shoulders relaxed at the thought of the precious woman.

"I heard you met Henry's grandson, Cameron." A slightly mischievous glint shone in Chester's eyes. "He's a nice young man."

"Yes. He seems to be." Hannah's cheeks warmed at the thought of Cameron.

"You two should go out sometime. I know a great restaurant over by the beach."

"Don't listen to Chester." Daphne paused while spraying her client's hair. "He's talking about a place where the waitstaff speaks like pirates. Great food, but unless you're into being greeted and served by swashbucklers, it's kind of strange."

Hannah chuckled. "I like pirate movies."

"See," Chester said as he smirked at Daphne. "Hannah would love it."

"Well," Daphne said. "A few months ago, I told my date about it, thinking we were going to some floozy place. I got all dressed up, and when we walked into the restaurant, Captain Mack Farrow greeted us at the door.

Date-man never again called for another date." She pointed her scissors at Chester. "Thanks to you."

"I thought you'd like the restaurant."

"Well, the food was good," Daphne said, "but I didn't realize my date had been in a boating accident when he was younger. He and his friends had been playing pirates when it happened. The boat sank."

"I'm sorry, Daphne," Chester said. "I had no idea."

"Date-man and his friends used a firework rocket as a cannon, and wound up blowing a hole in the boat's bottom."

Hannah cringed. "Was anyone hurt?"

"Nah, just the boat."

Chester groaned. "I thought something terrible had happened to one of the kids."

"No, but Date-Man acted like he was traumatized the whole time we were in that pirate-themed restaurant."

"I think you're better off without that guy," Chester said.

"Probably so. It's hard to find good men these days, especially for a woman in my age group. I keep searching through the online dating apps, but I don't want to date someone younger and have people call me a cougar. But why would they call women cougars, anyway? What does a big cat have to do with dating younger men?"

"I have no answer," Chester mumbled. He turned his gaze to Hannah. "Speaking of big cats. Have you seen Sir

Purrcevel around our fair town?"

"Sir Purrcevel?" Hannah finished with Chester's hair and removed the cape.

"He's one of those huge Maine cats, or a cross between a mountain lion and a Persian. No one's quite sure." Chester said as he stood. "He's ornery and smart as a whip, too. Rumor has it that he single-handedly or single-pawedly took down a stalker a few months ago."

Hannah grinned. "Is Sir Purrcevel available for hire?"

Chester's gaze turned serious. "You don't have a stalker, do you?"

She brushed the hair off the back of her chair. "I don't think so. It was just funny thinking about having a guard cat instead of a guard dog."

The bell over the door announced someone's arrival. Henry, along with a tall, muscular man, walked toward her.

"Yo, Valentino!" Daphne and Alma said in unison.

"Hannah," Henry said, "this is Valentino Bandoni."

The man looked like he'd stepped out of an action movie. She shook the strikingly handsome man's massive, outstretched hand. "Nice to meet you."

"Nice to meet you, too." Valentino's intense gaze seemed to pierce through her, revealing secrets of her past, yet somehow not making her feel threatened. "If you ever need help or protection, or someone to eliminate a problem, just call." He handed her his card.

"Okay, thanks."

The men stood around her, looking at her.

Hannah bit her lip. Did they know something she didn't know?

"Oh, let me pay you." Chester took out his wallet.

"You can pay Wanda up front." Hannah pointed to where her grinning boss stood.

Daphne nudged Valentino with her elbow. "You and your sweet wife need to stop by my place. I have your order ready for you."

"Great. Thank you. I'll see if we can't swing by this evening."

Daphne grinned at Hannah. "I make pottery in my spare time."

"She has some very nice ones on display at Knick Knacks Antique Store," Henry said.

His gaze turned serious as he stepped closer to Hannah. "I brought Valentino because I have some news about that gray car."

Chapter 17

"**W**hat did you find out about the vehicle?" Hannah's hands instinctively reached for the chair to steady herself.

"It was parked across the street," Henry said, "so I walked over to say hello. Even with the tinted windows, I could see someone sitting inside, so I tapped on the driver's side window. Instead of rolling it down, the car sped away."

"That is not normal behavior," Chester growled.

Henry gently guided her toward the back, while Chester and Valentino followed.

"I did get the license plate," Henry continued. "The car is from Pennsylvania. Do you know who it might have been?"

A creepy feeling slithered up Hannah's spine. "I don't think so."

"Then we'll take the information to the police station and find out who the car belongs to. I'll call in a few days to reschedule my appointment." Henry and Chester hurried away.

Valentino studied Hannah as though reading her discomfort. "Would you be willing to step into Wanda's office for a moment?"

Hannah tried not to take a step back. Why would he want her to go into the office with him?

Wanda hurried toward her. "You can trust Valentino. He's a good guy. If you want, I can come with you."

"Yes, please."

After they entered, Valentino closed the door. He waited until they sat before settling into the chair behind the desk. "Would you mind telling me what worries you about that car?" His gaze softened, a hint of warmth replacing the previous intensity. "I'm here to help."

"I'm not sure." Hannah placed her hands in her lap. Why would she reveal private information to someone she barely knew, particularly with her boss sitting next to her?

Then again, maybe a little information wouldn't hurt. "I saw a car like that sitting in my apartment's parking lot back in Pennsylvania. I thought someone might be watching me."

Wanda gasped. "You poor thing. Do you know who it might be? An old boyfriend?"

"I don't have any old boyfriends," Hannah whispered. At twenty-one, that fact was a little embarrassing.

"Why would you think someone might be watching you?" Valentino asked. "Hannah," he said gently, "I don't want to intrude, but if there's anything you can share, even a small detail, it might be helpful."

Hannah stared at her shoes. She felt silly for being paranoid. The car might have nothing to do with her.

Wanda placed her hand over Hannah's. "It's okay if you don't want to talk. Valentino's job is helping people with their problems. He's called the Eliminator. Not because he eliminates people, just problems."

Hannah did a quick glance at the man before staring again at her shoes. "Maybe it's nothing. Maybe I'm just imagining things. So, I don't want to bother you." Mama D would know what to do. "Can I make a call first?"

Both Valentino and Wanda nodded and stood.

"We'll give you some privacy," Wanda said as they left the room and closed the door.

Hannah pulled her phone out of her back pocket and placed a call to Mama D. When she answered, Hannah told her what was happening.

"Call Gloria. Right now," Mama D said. "She'll know about the people in town. I trust her. If she tells you it's okay, share anything you're comfortable with. Remember, God's got you. I love you."

"I love you, too. Thank you." Hannah ended the call and quickly dialed Gloria's number. Gloria vouched for Valentino, emphasizing that he had a proven track record of helping many people in town with their problems.

Feeling better about discussing the car and why she felt uneasy, Hannah let Valentino and Wanda back into the office.

Hannah sat on the seat's edge. "How much do you charge for your services?"

Valentino shook his head. "No charge. It's my honor to help."

"Okay. Thank you." Hannah struggled with how much to share.

"Take your time. Or do you want me to step out so you can talk privately to Valentino?" Compassion shone in Wanda's eyes.

"No, it's okay. I guess." If she opened up about her life, would they view her in a negative way? Admitting her mother was an adulteress, and that Hannah was the child of an illicit affair would be humiliating. She closed her eyes and said a silent prayer for help.

Feeling braver, Hannah met Valentino's gaze, and everything just flowed out. She told them the circumstances of her birth, her upbringing by Mama D, what she knew about Francesca and her death, and why Hannah was paranoid.

She couldn't believe she had shared her life story with them. However, instead of feeling ashamed or judged, Hannah felt as though a heavy burden had lifted off her shoulders. She wasn't to blame for how she was conceived or for Francesca's choices and mistakes.

Wanda patted Hannah's hand. "My goodness, you have had an interesting life. I'm so glad you moved here."

Valentino stood. "I appreciate your sharing. I'll keep

watch. I can drive you home after work."

"She's staying with me," Wanda said. "I don't want her to be alone until you find out about that car and we make sure she's safe."

Valentino gazed at Hannah. "Would you be okay staying here tonight, or possibly for a few days?"

She avoided making eye contact. If she were wrong about the car, she'd blabbed her life story for no good reason.

"I have a spare bedroom with a private bath," Wanda added. "It's already ready for visitors. We can hang out together. Come on. We'll have fun."

Staying with Wanda might be enjoyable. Hannah looked at her boss. "Okay. But just for tonight."

Valentino stood. "Did you walk to work or is your car out back?"

"I walked."

"I'm parked out back. Wanda, if you're not busy, why don't you ride with us to Hannah's place so she can get anything she needs?"

Wanda hugged Hannah's arm. "Come on, sweet thing. Let's go get your jammies so we can have a fun girls' night."

Five hours later, Hannah sank into the queen-sized bed in Wanda's guestroom and pulled the soft covers around her neck. After Wanda cooked a gourmet meal, they talked and laughed like they'd been friends for years, then finished the night watching a romantic comedy.

Hannah closed her eyes and let out a happy sigh. Maybe she'd been silly about the car thing. It was probably just a tourist visiting Crawdad Beach.

And as far as spilling the secrets of her past to her boss and someone called the Eliminator, it hadn't even been awkward or embarrassing.

She felt disconnected from her past, like she'd stepped inside a fiction novel. The mystery of Francesca's death, the disappearance of her mother's belongings, and the unknown location of her ashes, along with Johan's involvement, created a web of unanswered questions.

Hannah's eyes flew open. What if she were a character in a creepy crime story?

Chapter 18

Unable to sleep from overeating leftover pizza, Cameron rubbed his stomach.

Yawning, he opened his French doors and stepped out onto the balcony of his loft apartment that overlooked Main Street. Bright stars shone in the inky blackness of the moonless night.

Other than the Hotel de Crawdad, businesses were closed for the night, the silence broken only by the occasional chirp of crickets.

A subtle shift in the shadows across the street caught Cameron's attention. Instinctively, he moved back into his apartment, where he could watch without being seen.

A car cruised down the street, the headlights illuminating for a split second the silhouette of an enormous man. Not fat, but muscular and tall. Was he waiting for someone, or did he have evil intentions?

Cameron rubbed his neck. He needed to do something. Back in Texas, his guns were kept in a locked safe at his parents' house. Here, he had nothing he could use as a weapon. Not even a baseball bat.

He could take a stroll. Just pretend he was out for a

midnight walk. Maybe his showing up would scare the man off, or at least let him know he'd been seen.

Cameron softly closed his French doors and got ready. He put on his sneakers, jeans, and a dark t-shirt, then exited the back of the apartment building.

As quietly as possible, he crept through the dark alleyway until he came to the Main Street sidewalk.

Hoping the man wasn't watching, Cameron darted across the street and plastered himself against the brick building.

What was he thinking? He wanted to be noticed. Cameron drew up to his full height and stepped out of the shadows.

Whomp!

Cameron's face was smashed against the rough concrete sidewalk, his arms pinned behind him.

"Who are you and what are you doing?" asked a gruff voice.

With his mouth half-flattened against the gritty pavement, Cameron tried to act tough. "Who wants to know?"

He bit back a groan as the vise-like pressure on his arms and back intensified. "Okay. I'm Cameron Doss. I live here."

A beat passed. "Doss? You related to Henry?"

"Yes, he's my granddad."

A jolt threw Cameron to his feet, and he found himself

facing the largest, most muscular man he'd ever encountered outside of a football field.

The big man's eyes narrowed. "What are you doing out here, Cameron?"

Trying to be braver than he felt, he stood to his full height and still barely reached the man's shoulders. "I could ask the same thing. I saw you standing in the shadows."

The man looked him over. "Valentino Bandino. I'm keeping watch over Hannah." He motioned with his chin toward the beauty shop.

Cameron's pulse spiked. "Hannah Joy? Is she okay?"

"She's fine, but there's a car in the area she thinks might have followed her from Pennsylvania."

"That's disturbing." Cameron glanced at the beauty shop, then back at Valentino. "Why are you here and not outside where she lives?"

"She's staying at Wanda's place over the shop."

"Do you need help standing watch?"

"No."

At Valentino's firm statement, Cameron shoved his hands in his back pockets. "Could you at least tell me what the car looks like?"

"Gray four-door coupe with tinted windows."

Cameron glanced up and down the street, but didn't see any vehicles resembling that description. "I'll be on the lookout."

Valentino didn't respond, just kept focused on the beauty shop.

"Well, I'll let you get back to work." Cameron backed away, crossed the street, and returned to his apartment.

Why would someone be following Hannah, and why did she need a bodyguard?

Cameron rubbed his scratched-up face.

Who exactly was Hannah Joy?

"So, are you going to fill us in on what happened yesterday with Valentino?" Daphne asked.

Ready to start a new day, Hannah placed her purse in the bottom drawer of her station and turned to face Daphne and Alma's curious expressions. "I was worried a car followed me from Pennsylvania."

"What?" Alma laid a hand on her chest. "That would be creepy."

"Honey, you did the right thing talking to Valentino," Daphne said. "You don't mess with a stalker."

"I'm not sure what's going on. Maybe the car is only a look-alike."

"With Valentino on the job, you're in excellent hands." Daphne pointed out the front window. "Looks like he recruited some help."

A man sitting on a park bench across the street looked

surprisingly like the older version of the actor, Sean Connery. "Who is he?"

"That's Wilder Templeton. Ex-military. His wife, Stella, was, or still is, a cyber-spy. They sometimes work with Valentino," Daphne said, as though it wasn't a big deal. "This little town is filled with interesting people."

Alma chuckled as she readied her station. "You would be surprised what goes on in Crawdad Beach. Never a dull moment."

"Ladies," Wanda said as she walked toward the front. "Let's get this day started." She opened the door, and two ladies stepped inside and walked to Daphne and Alma's stations.

The bell over the door chimed, and Cameron rushed toward Hannah. His intense gaze swept over her. "You okay?"

"Yes, I'm fine."

He blew out a relieved breath. "Good."

"I don't have you scheduled for today."

"No, it's not that. I was worried about you." He handed her a piece of paper, stepped closer, and whispered in her ear. "I saw Valentino last night, so I'll be keeping a lookout for the car. Call me day or night if you need anything."

At Cameron's closeness, Hannah's cheeks burned, and a strange fluttering feeling erupted inside her stomach. "Thank you."

"You're welcome." He grinned as he backed away. "I'll see you soon."

After he left, Hannah sensed the curious stares of everyone in the shop. She took a quick glance. Sure enough, every person had a grin plastered on their faces as they stared at her.

Daphne nudged her with her shoulder. "I've heard Cameron's a good guy."

More heat rose to Hannah's cheeks. She gave a quick nod and shoved his number in her purse, then busied herself by taking out her supplies for the day. Hopefully, her customer would arrive soon so she could get to work.

It was both strange and comforting to have so many people concerned about her, especially Cameron. Regardless of what happened, she hoped they could be friends. Or maybe something more.

Hannah glanced back to where Wilder Templeton, the Sean Connery look-alike, was sitting.

As a man walked by, Wilder's head made an almost imperceptible, slow turn.

Wilder shot to his feet, seized the man, and hurled him against the building.

Chapter 19

"I can explain!" A man with one side of his face scratched, shouted as Wilder and Valentino shoved him inside the Beauty Shop.

With a collective whoosh, hair dryers and scissors fell silent, and all eyes turned towards the source of the commotion.

"Do you know who he is?" Valentino asked Hannah as he brought the man closer to where she stood.

To put some distance between them, Hannah stepped behind her stylist's chair. The man with dark hair, brown eyes, and a muscular physique accentuated by a tight polo shirt, appeared to be in his late twenties. She shook her head. "No. I've never seen him before."

"Of course she hasn't seen me," the guy said. "I'm supposed to be invisible."

"Your invisibility cloak isn't working," Daphne scoffed.

The man's gaze darted to Daphne. "She's not supposed to know that I'm watching her."

"Who sent you?" Valentino growled.

The guy looked away. "I can't say."

"Let's take him to the police station." Wilder stepped closer to the man.

"No, wait. I can't tell you. He doesn't want Hannah to know." The guy did a nervous glance around the room. "Can we go somewhere private to talk?"

Valentino motioned toward the back. "Hannah, if you're willing, I'd like you to join us."

Wanda grabbed hold of Hannah's arm. "I'm coming with you."

With faltering steps, Hannah followed behind the men to the office. Inside, she placed her back against the wall and stood beside Wanda.

Valentino closed the door and leaned in close, his face inches from the other man. "Talk."

"I'm not supposed to say. It's private."

"Let me take him for a little while," Wilder said, his voice calm but laced with an unsettling undertone. "We can have a private chat."

The guy's gaze darted back and forth between the men. He muttered curse words before looking at Valentino. "Mr. Rauchmann hired me."

Hannah gasped. "Johan?"

"No. His son. Augustine."

"His son? But, why?"

"Francesca died in a car wreck."

"We're aware of that fact," Valentino said. "What's that got to do with Hannah?"

The guy swiped away the sweat beading on his brow. "Mr. Rauchmann wasn't sure it was an accident, and that Hannah might be in danger."

Her mother *had* been murdered. Hannah's legs gave way beneath her as she fought to stay upright.

Wanda and Valentino steadied Hannah and helped her to a chair.

Valentino turned back to the guy. "What does Mr. Rauchmann think happened?"

"I'm not sure. Just that he wanted Hannah to be kept safe."

Wilder stepped closer to him. "How do we know you're telling the truth?"

Fumbling in his back pocket, the guy took out his wallet and held up a card. "My name is Phillip Winship. I'm a private bodyguard. Look, you've got to give me a break. This is my first assignment outside of Pennsylvania. I can't mess this up."

Valentino and Wilder exchanged a look, a silent glance.

"You can't be on 24/7 duty." Wilder grabbed the card. "Is someone working with you?"

"Yeah, he's back at the hotel sleeping. I've got days. He's the night guy."

Wilder took out his cell phone. "Let me make a few calls and check out Phillip's story."

"Don't get me in trouble."

Wilder shot a sharp glance at Phillip before stepping out of the room, the door clicking shut behind him.

Valentino's silent gaze stayed directed at Phillip. "My friend has connections. He will discover whether you are telling the truth."

Phillip ran a hand through his hair. "How do I know you guys aren't the ones making trouble for Hannah?"

A low, rumbling growl vibrated from deep within Valentino's chest as he stepped in front of Phillip. "We are here to protect her, and that includes you if your story doesn't check out."

In the big man's presence, Phillip seemed to shrink. "If we're on the same side, shouldn't we be working together?"

Valentino crossed his arms over his massive chest. "We'll see."

"Can we go now?" Wanda asked Valentino. "I'm sure you can handle whatever comes next."

"Yes, we'll handle it from here." He helped Hannah to her feet and closed the door after they left.

Once out of the office, Wanda embraced Hannah. "Are you okay? Do you want to go upstairs and rest for a while?"

Tears welled in Hannah's eyes as she stayed in Wanda's gentle hug. "I'll be okay. Working might be helpful. I have someone coming in a few minutes."

"I can take care of your clients," Wanda said.

Hannah stepped out of the embrace and rubbed the moisture out of her eyes. "Thanks. I can handle it."

The unsettling, bizarre nature of the whole thing left her mind barely able to process. It didn't make sense that Johan's son wanted to keep her safe.

Why would he care?

A sudden, terrifying thought crossed her mind. Was she in danger from Johan or his wife?

Chapter 20

"You've got to fill us in," Daphne said, as she and Alma huddled around Hannah.

Hannah kept her voice low. "The man might be a bodyguard sent to protect me."

"A bodyguard?" Daphne scrunched closer. "If he's a bodyguard, why isn't he wearing dark glasses and a suit with one of those earpiece things?"

"That's just in the movies," Alma said matter-of-factly.

"Likely story," Daphne muttered. "Wait, Hannah, why would you need a bodyguard?"

"She's probably famous," Alma said. "The daughter of a European king who escaped to America to live like a normal person."

A look of utter bewilderment crossed Daphne's face as she shot Alma a confused look. "You have *got* to stop reading those romance novels."

"You have to admit, Hannah has a sweet voice, but she doesn't talk like us."

Daphne groaned. "She moved here from the North. She hasn't picked up the proper way of speaking Southern yet."

"So, I'm right. Hannah came from a northern kingdom." Alma grinned.

"Oh, good grief." Daphne held up her hands. "How many princesses have you met in real life?"

"Just one. Hannah."

Hannah puffed out a laugh. "I'm definitely not a princess, but thanks for the fun thought."

"Well, whatever your story, we're glad you're here." Alma patted Hannah's arm. "And if you need a bodyguard, my oldest son's a big strapping young man who would be glad to help."

Daphne shook her head. "Hannah already has Valentino and Wilder, and maybe that other guy." She turned a questioning gaze to Hannah. "How many bodyguards do you need? Maybe you are a princess."

"Okay, ladies." Wanda joined them. "Give the girl some breathing room. Your next clients will be here soon."

Daphne and Alma continued discussing the possibility that Hannah might be a princess as they returned to their stations.

Wilder, carrying a laptop, rushed inside and hurried to the back office. The door slammed shut.

Hannah busied herself with rearranging items in her work area. She should have stayed in the office to find out what was happening.

Her mother's murder was likely the work of Johan or perhaps Johan's wife, both of whom might want her dead. Hannah sighed. Being the runaway daughter of a king would be a much better story than her reality.

"Good morning." Henry Doss stood next to her.

She hadn't even noticed he'd come inside. "Morning."

He grinned. "I believe I'm your next appointment."

"Oh, I'm sorry." Hannah tried to refocus on her work. "Yes, let's get your hair washed."

"I was hoping you would say that." Henry followed her to the sink area. "How have you been?"

She mustered up a smile. "Fine."

His skeptical gaze revealed his doubt. "Please let me know if I can do anything."

"Thank you." Hannah wrapped Henry's shoulders in a towel and snapped on a cape. "I'm sure everything will be fine." At least she hoped so.

She gently adjusted his head for a comfortable wash. After checking the water temperature, she wet his hair and then applied a generous amount of shampoo.

Hannah slid her fingers into the warm, soapy lather as she massaged Henry's scalp. Mama D was a wonderful stand-in mom, and her family had been a blessing, but why couldn't she have had a sweet dad and granddad like Henry?

With Johan's son sending bodyguards, what did he think might happen to her? She wasn't a threat to anyone.

Unless something else was going on.

Hannah refocused her thoughts, finished washing Henry's hair, then took him to her station.

He smiled as he sat in the stylist's chair. "My contented scalp and I thank you for the wash and massage."

"You're welcome." She clipped on the cape. "Is there a specific cut you prefer?"

"Whatever you think is best."

His hair needed minimal work, so she gave him a quick trim with clippers on the back and a shaping with scissors.

"Hannah." Valentino motioned for her to join him. "When you have time." His gaze swung to the front. "Wanda, I'd like you to join us."

"Is everything okay?" Henry gazed at her in the mirror.

"I hope so." Hannah removed his cape, then dusted off his neck and shoulders.

"My hair looks great, and my scalp is tingling with happiness."

Hannah grinned at the sweet compliment. "My pleasure. You can pay up front with Wanda."

"Call anytime if I can be of service. Oh, by the way, Cameron said to tell you hello."

Her cheeks warmed at the mention of Henry's grandson. "Tell him hello for me."

The corners of Henry's eyes crinkled with his smile. "I will do that."

While Henry walked to the front to pay, Hannah took a deep breath and made her way to the office.

Wanda's quick steps sounded on the floor as she came beside her. "I'm with you. Don't worry."

Hannah sent up a prayer for help. She sensed that whatever she discovered, her life would probably change.

Standing near the desk, Phillip and Wilder greeted her as the women took their seats.

Valentino closed the door, sat behind the desk, and moved a laptop to where Hannah could see the screen. "Rauchmann Industries released a press statement this morning."

Hannah skimmed through the information. Effective immediately, Johan Rauchmann was no longer with the company. His son, Augustine, had been appointed president and CEO. Johan's wife, Genevieve, assumed the role of chairman of the board.

Hoping for answers and clarity, Hannah looked at the men. "What does this mean?"

Wilder took a knee beside her, his eyes filled with concern. "Through my security contacts, we discovered that Johan Rauchmann was arrested this morning by Interpol. He's in their custody and on the way to France. Johan has been charged with murder, drug-trafficking, and money-laundering."

Hannah's hand shot to her chest, her heart pounding. "Johan was involved in all of those things? But if he was arrested for murder, did that mean?"

"Yes." Wilder gave a quick nod. "I'm sorry, Hannah. Johan paid a man to sabotage the brakes on your mother's car. That man is in the custody of the Pennsylvania police."

Chapter 21

Before he went to work, Cameron took a quick shower and got ready.

Three days had passed since Hannah had left Crawdad Beach. Although he didn't know her that well, and they weren't dating, he missed her.

He ran downstairs and went straight to the beauty shop.

Wanda, her broom pausing mid-sweep, looked up and smiled. "Hi Cameron. I'm sorry, I still don't have any news about Hannah. She has responded to texts but hasn't said when she'll return."

Cameron rubbed his hand across his neck. "You think she will?"

"I hope so."

"You still won't tell me anything else about what happened?"

"Just that her mom's death wasn't an accident. I'll let Hannah tell you, since it's her story. Why don't you send her a text and let her know you're thinking about her?"

"Yeah, okay." Cameron thanked Wanda, then returned to his apartment and slumped onto the couch.

Even Valentino hadn't told him any other information other than that Hannah was now safe.

Cameron couldn't imagine how she must be feeling after losing her mother and finding out the death wasn't an accident. If something like that happened to his mom, he didn't know what he'd do.

He wasn't sure what to say if he texted or called. What if he said something that made things worse?

For now, he'd continue praying for Hannah. And maybe he could think of something to say that was nice and caring enough that she'd return to Crawdad Beach.

Hannah sat next to Mama D in the backyard of her son's house. The ladies at the beauty shop were covering until she got back. No one mentioned a timeframe for her return.

A bee gathering pollen danced around potted flowers on the patio. A bird sang in the brightly blooming crepe myrtles that ran along the back fence. High above, fluffy white clouds, like cotton balls, drifted across the early evening blue sky.

The world continued spinning, and life went on regardless of what happened in people's lives.

Hannah wrapped a strand of her long hair around her finger.

Valentino and Wilder had uncovered more information from their network of security professionals and cyber spies. Before Francesca died, she'd sent Jonah's wife, Genevieve, a packet with a letter asking for forgiveness, along with papers and files documenting Johan's illegal activities.

With the information Genevieve received, she was the one who turned Johan over to the authorities. She'd endured years of Johan's manipulation and infidelity.

Hannah sighed. The events still felt disjointed and confusing, as if she were in a strange nightmare or one of those television true-life crime dramas. "My life doesn't feel real."

"I know, Baby," Mama D said. "You've been through so much in your young life."

"But I didn't. Not really. You gave me a loving home and a great childhood. I'm sad about what could have been, but it's hard to miss Francesca when I barely knew her. As for Johan, it's probably a good thing we never met. Still, it's super embarrassing having parents like that."

"They are your parents, but what they did does not reflect on you. They are responsible for their actions. You are your own person. And the best thing about their union was you, Hannah," Mama D said with a gentle smile.

"As for your father," she continued. "God is your true Father, who knitted you together in your mother's womb. He is the one who brought you into this world and into my life. You are a blessing, sweet girl, to me and my family."

"Thank you for those reminders and sweet words." Hannah's lip trembled. "Please let me help you financially. You've done so much for me over the years."

"No, baby," Mama D said. "You don't need to do that. Francesca paid well for your care. I have everything I need and could ever want. You wait here."

Mama D groaned as she got to her feet, shooing away Hannah's help. "I'll be right back."

Hannah stretched her legs out in front of her. The melody of a Christian song echoed in her mind, its lyrics about God hearing the cries, sending an army to find and rescue.

She glanced at the sky.

Had God rescued her?

Even with all she'd learned about her parents, Hannah sensed God's nearness. Mama D hadn't only been her caretaker; she'd been her friend and her true mother.

Yes, God had rescued her.

"Baby," Mama D handed her a large white envelope. "Open it and tell me what you think."

Hannah gave her a curious glance. "Please don't tell me it's something else about Francesca or Johan."

"No. This is something new."

Slipping open the envelope, Hannah withdrew official papers.

Hannah gasped at the already filled-out forms from the State of South Carolina—Certificate of Adoption.

Happy tears blurred her vision as she looked up. "You want to adopt me?"

Mama D's sweet chuckle reverberated in her chest. "Yes. If you're okay with this, my children, grandchildren, and I all agree that you should officially become part of the Samson family."

"Yes!" Hannah squealed as she vaulted to her feet and gave Mama D the biggest hug she could. "A million times, yes! Thank you. Thank you. Thank you!"

Chapter 22

Munching on the last yummy bites of a cinnamon roll Hannah had bought at Rolling in the Dough Bakery, she made her way towards the beauty shop.

Despite her excitement at joining the Samson family, the pull of Crawdad Beach proved too strong. The little town already felt like home and was located close enough to see Mama D and the family anytime Hannah wanted.

Plus, Cameron had been calling late in the evenings and checking on her, asking if there was anything he could do to help. Each time he called, they talked for hours, and he always left off saying he'd pray for her. Cameron possessed a sweetness and warmth that touched her heart, unlike any guy she'd ever met.

Ready to get back to work and start her day, Hannah wiped her hands on a napkin, then opened the beauty shop door.

Daphne, Alma, and Wanda raced to her, showering Hannah with hugs, comforting words about her mother's death, and excited comments about her return.

Hannah let out a little laugh. She was only gone for a few days.

Wanda whispered in her ear. "Guess who's been coming by the beauty shop?"

Hannah didn't have a clue. "Who?"

"Cameron Doss. He came by every morning hoping you'd returned."

"Really? That's so sweet." With her heart happy dancing in her chest, Hannah placed her backpack purse in the bottom drawer of her station.

"Speaking of your admirer," Wanda motioned toward the front window.

Cameron stepped into the building. His eyes met Hannah's, and a warm smile spread across his face. "You're back." He hurried toward her. "How are you doing?"

"I'm fine. Thank you for the calls."

"My pleasure. I'm glad you're back." Their eyes locked, and the world seemed to fade away, leaving only the two of them.

"Love is in the air," Daphne sang as she sashayed past.

Cameron cleared his throat and grinned at Hannah. "Got time to give me a haircut?"

"I'm not sure." She fumbled with her phone to check her schedule.

"You've got time!" Wanda shouted from the front.

Her cheeks on fire, Hannah motioned for Cameron to follow her to the sinks.

"My family is grateful you've been cutting my hair."

Cameron positioned himself in the chair. "My aunt said I was looking like a shaggy dog before you moved to town."

"You weren't that bad." Hannah put a towel around his shoulders and snapped the cape on. "More like a cute shaggy dog."

"Cute, huh?"

She stifled her grin as she checked the water temperature.

"Ever had anything funny happen at work?"

Hannah wet his hair and lathered in the shampoo. "At the place I worked in Pennsylvania, a lady came in with a scarf on her head. When she took it off, her hair was bright, neon green."

"Was it St. Patrick's Day?"

"Nope. Not even close. The lady had used a product she'd found under her sink that was probably twenty years old. Her hair did *not* react well."

"Obviously." He chuckled. "Any other stories?" His eyes were getting a relaxed, dreamy look as she continued massaging his scalp.

"There was another lady who brought a bag full of her hair. She hadn't been truthful about using bleach when a beautician worked on her, and all the woman's hair had fallen out."

"So, what you're telling me is I should always be truthful and very kind to my hairdresser."

"That's right." Hannah gave him a sly smile. "Consider

the consequences before you provoke someone holding sharp objects who can dramatically, even terrifyingly, alter your appearance."

Cameron laughed. "I will keep that in mind."

She rinsed his hair, wrapped the towel around his head, and led him to her stylist's chair.

He stopped beside her. "Could I take you to dinner this evening? Chester told me about a great seafood restaurant by the beach. Then, if you'd like, we could take a walk by the ocean."

Fluttering butterflies rose inside her stomach. Hannah nodded. "I'd love to." She took out her scissors and clippers. "So, did Chester tell you anything else about the restaurant?"

"No, only that they have great food. Chester said he'd recommended it many times to people around town."

Hannah bit back her laugh as she used the clippers to trim the back of Cameron's hair. Chester had probably suggested the one with pirates.

A subtle shaking of Daphne's shoulders, along with a soft chuckle, showed that she was having the same thought. Even Alma was grinning.

Between being in Cameron's company and the possibility of eating with a waitstaff dressed as swashbucklers, Hannah knew she was in for a very memorable evening.

Still embarrassed about the restaurant Cameron had taken Hannah to, he walked next to her along the near-empty beach. "I'm sorry about the restaurant. I did not know we'd be served by pirates."

"I keep telling you, it was great." Hannah smiled. "I loved it. The food was terrific, and our server was hilarious. Besides that, I had heard that was where Chester sent people."

"You knew? No wonder you could converse with the servers in pirate speak."

Her eyes sparked with mischief as she glanced at him. "Aye, me matey. There be an online pirate translator for landlubbers."

"You're kidding?"

"No, really. All you have to do is type in a sentence, and it will translate it into pirate speak for you."

Cameron gave her a look of admiration. "You are a woman of many talents. With your skills at pirate speak, masterful massage and shampoo techniques, and expert hair cutting abilities, you are a true artist."

She stopped and faced him. "Aw, thank you. That's sweet of you to say."

Hannah's kind eyes and gentle smile captivated him as a gentle breeze caused her long hair to dance around her face. She was beautiful, inside and out.

Cameron's gaze fell to her lips, then back up to her gorgeous green eyes, which widened.

Hannah licked her lips and crossed her arms. "Do you miss Texas?"

It took Cameron a few seconds to focus. "Yeah, sometimes. But being in the same town as my granddad, aunts, uncles, and cousins is great. The family gathers every few weeks at my cousin David's house to grill hamburgers."

"How about you? Do you miss Pennsylvania?"

"Not really. Mama D lives within driving distance."

"Mama D?"

"She raised me and is going to be my official mother. I mean, as soon as the adoption papers make their way through the court system."

Cameron couldn't hide his surprise. "You're getting adopted?"

"Yes, now that my mother is dead and my father is," Hannah hesitated for a moment, "well, he's out of the picture." She reached into her purse, took out her phone, and showed Cameron a photo of her standing with a group of people. Everyone was smiling with their arms linked.

Cameron grinned at her excitement. "Nice looking family. Looks like everyone's happy."

"I know; it's great. God's really blessed me. My name will be Hannah Joy Samson."

He held out his hand. "Miss Samson, it's nice to meet

you."

She shook Cameron's hand. "Thank you, Mr. Doss."

He held Hannah's soft hand in his. She gave his fingers a quick squeeze and then took a few steps before turning to make sure he followed.

Cameron grinned as he caught up. They continued walking as the waves moved gently against the shore.

Hannah's gaze found his for a split second before she turned away. "You don't have a problem with my family, do you?"

"No, of course not. Why would I do that?"

"I have a different skin color than they do."

"True, but why would that matter?"

"I know racism exists. I've seen it in action too many times against me, Mama D, and her family. I mean my family. I've never understood the concept. There are good and bad people of every nationality. Why hate someone based on the color of their skin?"

"Exactly. You've met my granddad, Henry. He's white, but my grandmother was Asian, and for some weird reason, some people had a problem with that. There is only one race, the human race."

With a piercing shriek, a seagull swooped down and dive-bombed a small crab. The little guy held high his tiny but menacing pincers, ready for battle.

Cameron lunged forward, snatching the crab just in time. "I've got you."

The seagull let out a loud, angry cry before flying away.

"Thank you for saving him," Hannah said.

Cameron held the crab gingerly as the little pincers snapped in displeasure. "I'm not so sure he's as appreciative."

Walking to the water's edge, Cameron released the little crab, watching as it disappeared into the ocean. "Not even a thank you." He playfully grumbled.

Hannah leaned toward him and gave him a kiss on his cheek. "Thank you."

He grinned. "For what?"

"Rescuing the crab, and for what you said about my family."

Cameron gently threaded his fingers through hers. "Anytime you need a crab rescue, a kind word about work, family, or yourself—day or night—just give me a call. I'm your man."

Chapter 23

Still smiling from the fantastic evening, Hannah unlocked her door and turned toward Cameron. "Thank you for a wonderful evening."

"My pleasure. I had a great time." He took her hand in his, his touch sending a shiver down her spine. "I'd like to see you again."

"I'd like that."

Cameron stepped closer and gently pulled her into his arms.

She fell into his warm embrace. His arms around her were the perfect combination of gentleness and strength.

With a tender touch, he pressed his lips against hers. His kisses were light and sweet. As they pulled apart, a breathless gasp escaped. Who knew kissing could be so lovely?

Cameron smiled. "Nice, Miss Samson, very nice."

She fanned her face. "You're not too bad yourself, Mr. Doss." Not that she had that much practice.

He kissed her again, a slow, tender kiss. With a moan, he stepped back. "I'd better go."

Hannah, feeling a touch lightheaded, nodded. "I don't

want you to, but you probably should." Mama D's warnings about letting things get out of hand echoed in her mind.

But one more kiss probably wouldn't hurt.

By the time Cameron left, Hannah felt like she was floating as she got ready for bed. She touched her lips that still tingled from his kisses.

Cameron's hands had never roamed, and his kisses were soft, never crossing a line. She'd never met a man as nice as he was, and definitely not as handsome and sweet.

For all the weird, crazy, disturbing things she'd been through, she had so much to be thankful for. Being adopted by Mama D and spending time with Cameron had been amazing.

Hannah sank into her bed, pulled the covers to her neck, and gazed at the ceiling. "Thank You, God."

Cameron returned to his apartment and stepped out onto his balcony. He wouldn't be able to sleep for a while, not after being with Hannah.

Not only was she beautiful, but she had a great sense of humor and could communicate without taking her phone out every few minutes to take selfies or check social media.

One thing troubled him, though.

Other than a brief mention of Hannah's mother's death and her father being out of the picture, she didn't seem upset.

Had she grieved, or was she just stuffing her emotions?

Cameron rubbed the back of his neck. Maybe he should have said something, so that Hannah knew he was sorry for what she'd been through.

Ivy would have wailed for months, posting all over social media about how terrible her life was. But with her, it hadn't taken much for her to complain. She even tried to get people to boycott a coffee shop because she didn't receive what she thought was the correct amount of cream in her coffee.

Hopefully, Hannah wasn't anything like Ivy. From the conversations he had with Hannah, Mama D had instilled in her a love for God that gave her inner strength.

Cameron stared up at the moonlit sky. Whatever happened next, he needed God's wisdom and guidance.

He'd made a mess of his life by getting involved with the wrong person before; he did not want to make another mistake.

As soon as Hannah stepped into the beauty shop, Wanda hurried toward her. "So, how was your date?"

Hannah grinned as she walked to her station to get ready. "It was very nice."

Wanda got a dreamy look. "Cameron is such a nice young man. Handsome, too."

With a mischievous grin, Daphne leaned against Hannah's stylist chair. "Did you see any pirates?"

"Yes, that was so much fun."

"You enjoyed it?"

"Aye, I be thar love fer pirates."

Daphne tilted her head. "What?"

"Yes, I love pirates," Hannah grinned. "That was the pirate-speak translation. I don't like nasty real-life pirates, but the restaurant-themed place was great."

"The food is fantastic," Alma said. "My husband loves to go there. He even bought an eyepatch to wear when we visit and calls himself Dead-Eye Davey."

Wanda chuckled as she handed the ladies a printed-out schedule for the day. "Hannah, would you be willing to train us one evening after work with your massage techniques?"

"Sure. That'd be fun."

"Yes!" Daphne pumped a fist into the air. "I can finally work on the cute man who comes in every month when he visits his sister."

"If you ask me, he's already interested in you," Alma said.

"Well, if he is, he needs to get his tail in gear and ask

me out. I'm not a spring chicken like Princess Hannah. I'm more of a well-seasoned chick."

The bell above the door chimed, announcing someone's arrival.

Gloria's face held an amused expression as she stood next to an older couple. "Hannah, I have someone who wants to meet you."

Chapter 24

Hannah stared at the vaguely familiar couple as they walked toward her.

Where had she seen them before?

"I can't believe we finally found you," the lady whispered, her voice choked with sobs, tears streaming down her face.

The man was also teary-eyed as he stared at Hannah, as if she were a ghost. "We've been looking for you for years."

Gloria grinned at the couple. "Hannah, I want you to meet Francesca's parents and your grandparents, Brent and Melissa Joy."

Hannah's legs gave way, and she reached out to steady herself against her stylist chair. They were the couple in the photos.

The woman, with her lined face and kind eyes, bore a striking resemblance to Francesca, while the man, although bearing the marks of time, remained handsome.

"We didn't know what had happened to you." Her grandmother took a halting step closer. "We searched and searched, but you vanished without a trace. It wasn't until we received a letter from Francesca asking for our forgiveness that we knew what had happened. She also wrote telling us where to find Dorthea Samson, and your Mama D led us here."

Hannah stared speechless, unable to process what she was seeing and hearing.

"Well, don't just stand there; get a group hug," Daphne said.

Amidst the sobs and tears of everyone around, Hannah's grandparents enveloped her in a comforting, long-awaited embrace.

"Hannah, why don't you use my office?" Wanda said as she swiped away her tears. "We'll cover for you."

The hours flew by in a blur of laughter, tears, and shared stories. Hannah discovered that the house she had visited that day was the correct one. The young couple she thought were the homeowners were relatives. The man was Francesca's younger brother, which meant Hannah had an uncle.

"By the way, we love your adopted mother," Hannah's grandmother said.

"You don't mind my taking her name?"

"Of course not. Dorothea raised you, and it's clear from our meeting that she dearly loves you. As much as we wished we could have been there for you, God knew exactly where you needed to be to keep you safe. You will always be Hannah Joy, even if your name now ends in

Samson."

"You are our found joy." Hannah's grandfather's voice trembled with emotion as a warm smile lit up his face.

Chapter 25

A cricket serenade filled the late evening as Cameron sat beside Hannah on her screened-in porch. "That's wild that you finally met your grandparents."

"It was incredible. They are super, super sweet. Even though they took care of me while I was a baby, I don't have any memories of them. We talked for hours, and I can't wait to see them again."

"I can't believe all you've been through."

"It doesn't seem real. It's more made for TV stuff than my story. Mama D and her family. I mean, my family gave me a great life."

"Didn't you miss having a mother and father?"

"Not really. Mama D was my mother. I guess there were a few times I wondered what it would have been like, but how can I miss what I never had? Mama D's family was the best."

Cameron glanced at Hannah. How could she talk as though what she'd gone through wasn't a big deal?

Her mother had been murdered, her father was in prison, and her grandparents hadn't been part of her life for almost twenty years.

Cameron knew other people who would cry, whine, and wail, their anger and bitterness lingering for days, weeks, months, or even years. Which only made themselves and everyone around them miserable.

He kept his tone gentle. "Do you think you've processed your mother's death?"

"Maybe?" Hannah looked lost in thought as she wound a strand of her long hair around her finger. "I hate what happened to Francesca, but from her letters, it sounds like she got right with God before she was killed. It's a comfort to know I'll see her again, and when I do, she'll be happy."

"Was she not happy?" Cameron asked.

"I don't think so. Francesca pursued the wrong things, and definitely the wrong person. I think she got in so deep she didn't know how to escape."

"You sure are wise for someone so young."

Hannah puffed out a scoff. "Not really. Mama D is the wise one. She said to keep focused on the eternal instead of the temporary. And that we have two choices when something bad happens."

Cameron gave her a curious look. "Two choices?"

"Yep. We can either pray and give it to God and trust Him, or we can whine and complain. If we pray and give it to God, we can have God's peace. If we whine and complain, we won't have peace."

"Sounds too easy."

"It's not," Hannah said. "Sometimes releasing troubles to God feels like a wrestling match, a struggle to trust Him. Mama D said God knows and understands that life hurts. There's a time to weep, a time for grief, yet we have to remember God loves us, is in control, and will help us through whatever we go through."

Cameron spent a moment processing Hannah's statements. His life would have been much easier if he'd given his troubles sooner to God.

With a worried look and a soft touch, Hannah's hand rested on his arm. "I didn't mean to sound churchy."

"No, you didn't. You shared something I needed to hear."

"I guess I said all that because I needed a reminder. It would be so easy to spiral into a pity party."

He knew all too well how that went. He'd been in a pity party spiral for months after the Ivy situation. And Ivy had excelled at pity parties, whether real or imagined, to get as many social media followers as possible.

Cameron sighed. "Some people live their lives only thinking about the negative things that happened, letting those memories poison their present."

"Right." Hannah turned toward him, her eyes softening as she looked at him. "I don't want that to happen to me. I can't change the past. I can't change what Francesca did, or my father did, or any of that stuff. I've got today. I want to live in the moment. And right now,

I'm so glad I'm here with you."

Cameron leaned in and kissed her lips. "I'm glad I'm here with you, too."

Hannah couldn't stop smiling. She and Cameron had been officially dating for seven months. He'd taken her to a fancy restaurant with a romantic atmosphere. No pirates this time.

Her fingers laced with his, they walked along the shoreline.

A seagull ambled toward them and tilted its head. With a screech, it flew away.

Cameron huffed. "I wonder if that bird was the one I kept from getting the crab."

"He did seem a bit angry. But don't worry, there is a crab out there in the ocean telling the tale of his rescue by the valiant man who saved him from the beaks of death."

Cameron let out a soft laugh as he gazed her way. "I've never been called valiant before. I'll accept the compliment. Thank you."

"My pleasure." She gave him a playful nudge. "I can't believe we've dated for seven months. It's gone so fast. I've had a wonderful time."

"It has been great." He stopped, brought their joined hands to his lips, and kissed the back of her hand. "I love you, Hannah."

"I love you, too." Hannah leaned in to get a kiss.

They'd been declaring their love for one another after the first month of dating.

She would never stop loving hearing Cameron say those words, or being able to tell them back to the man she loved.

Long shadows stretched across the warm sand as they continued walking. A gentle breeze carried the scent of salt and sea.

Hannah took a deep breath. Cameron and she had spent almost every evening and weekend together. They attended church on Sunday mornings and then would have lunch with Cameron's family.

Trips to see her grandparents and Mama D. were frequent, filled with laughter and the warm embrace of countless hugs.

Clients at the beauty shop loved that Hannah taught the other ladies her massage techniques. They now had more customers than they could handle. Wanda was even thinking of hiring another beautician.

Life couldn't get much better. Most days, she felt as though she were walking on air.

Cameron led Hannah away from the waves and turned to face her, a warm smile on his lips. "I love you, Hannah."

"I love you, too."

"I am very grateful God brought you to Crawdad Beach, and that we found one another. I want us to be together forever." He fumbled with something in his pocket, then went down on one knee.

Hannah's heart pounded as Cameron held out a beautiful marquise-cut diamond ring.

"Hannah Joy Samson, will you marry me?"

Tears of pure joy streamed down her face. "Yes! I love you, Cameron Doss."

Rising to his feet, he pulled her close, the scent of his subtle cologne filling her senses as he gave her a kiss she'd never forget.

The End

Thank you for reading

A Found Joy

Lisa Buffaloe

Acknowledgments

Above all else, I am deeply grateful to God for the immeasurable gift of salvation, the countless times He rescues those in need, and the promise of eternal life in His loving family.

Dennis, thank you for being a wonderful, loving husband, and for your prayers, support, and encouragement. I'm so thankful we found each other.

Patricia (Pacjac) Carroll, thank you again for your insightful critiques, helpful feedback, and for making the writing process loads of fun.

JoAnn Durgin, thank you again for creating another beautiful cover. You are a sweet blessing.

Jack Foster, thank you again for your creative Crawdad drawings used throughout the series. (Readers, please visit Jack at jackfosterart.com)

Thank you for taking the time to read *A Found Joy.* I am very grateful to each of you.

If you enjoyed the novel, would you be so kind as to leave a positive review and share it with your friends?

Thank you!

About the Author

Lisa Buffaloe is a happily married mom, speaker, and multi-published author. She loves spending time with God, her sweet hubby, studying the Bible, writing, and enjoying nature.

Please visit Lisa at https://lisabuffaloe.com, Facebook, X(Twitter), Instagram (buffaloelisa), Goodreads, and Amazon https://amzn.to/4ltfEBA

Books by Lisa
Fiction

Readers can read each book individually or as part of the series.

Crawdad Beach Series

Visible, yet Hidden
Running to Grace
Crystal's Journey Home
A Baker's Heart
Stella's Heart Code
River Steps Free
Mia Lets Go
A New Paige
Running from Shame
Elise's New Song
A Found Joy

Hope and Grace Series

Nadia's Hope
Prodigal Nights
Writing Her Heart
The Discovery Chapter
Open Lens

Stand-alone novels

The Masterpiece Beneath
The Fortune
Grace for the Char-Baked

Non-Fiction

Float by Faith
Heart and Soul Medication
Time with The Timeless One
The Forgotten Resting Place
Present in His Presence
We Were Meant for Paradise
One Lit Step: Devotions for your journey
The Unnamed Devotional
Flying on His Wings
Unfailing Treasures
No Wound Too Deep For The Deep Love of Christ
Living Joyfully Free Devotional (Volumes 1 & 2)

Lisa Buffaloe

A Found Joy

Lisa Buffaloe

www.ingramcontent.com/pod-product-compliance
Lightning Source LLC
Chambersburg PA
CBHW070330130626
46556CB00007B/2791